A *Life* IN THE COUNTRY

The Unknown Country: Canada and Her People
The Hollow Men
The Fraser
The Incredible Canadian: A Candid Portrait of Mackenzie
   King, His Works, His Times, and His Nation
Canada's Lonely Neighbour
The Struggle for the Border
Canada: Tomorrow's Giant
Mr. Prime Minister: 1867–1964
Macdonald to Pearson: The Prime Ministers of Canada
Western Windows
Canada: A Year of the Land
The Far Side of the Street
Uncle Percy's Wonderful Town
The Unfinished Country: To Canada with Love and Some
   Misgivings

A LIFE IN THE COUNTRY

BRUCE HUTCHISON

Douglas & McIntyre
Vancouver/Toronto

Douglas & McIntyre Ltd.
1615 Venables Street
Vancouver, British Columbia V5L 2H1

Canadian Cataloguing in Publication Data

Hutchison, Bruce, 1901–
   A life in the country

   ISBN 0-88894-620-1

   1. Hutchison, Bruce, 1901–   2. Journalists—Canada
—Biography. 3. Country life—British Columbia—
Vancouver Island. I. Title.
PN4913.H87A3 1988   070′.92′4   C88-091481-5

Design by Barbara Hodgson
Illustrations by Marion Dahl
Typeset by The Typeworks
Printed and bound in Canada by D.W. Friesen & Sons Ltd.

*For Dorothy, Joan, Robert and
all my companions of the soil
and the wilderness*

CONTENTS

FELLOW CREATURES
OF THE SOIL

Fellow Creatures of the Soil

IN THE AUTUMN of 1924, when I had started to fence a dozen acres of cheaply purchased meadow, rock and trees outside Victoria, my closest neighbour, from half a mile distant, found me digging holes, inserting heavy cedar posts and regretting a fatal mistake. Harry Snape brought good advice, but he came too late. For I was committed beyond rescue to the country life that urban dwellers envy and fortunately escape.

Besides his advice, Snape carried under his ragged military overcoat the disjointed barrel and stock of a shotgun for the illegal slaughter of sitting pheasants. From his lips, as long as I knew him, dangled a moist, hand-rolled cigarette. He kept trying to light it with innumerable matches and usually failed. Now, failing again, he sat down on a stump and, in a whining cockney accent, uttered the Lord's name in vain and some lewd adjectives peculiar to London's East End.

"Yer'll not like it 'ere," he warned me. "Nobody likes it 'ere. She's a bitch an' no mistake, a bloody bitch. Nothin' to do, nothin' to see, nowheres to go."

"Why," I asked, "did you come?"

"Because I was a goddamn fool. But I was through wiv the army an' they give me a pension you could put in your eye an' all the papers said go to the colonies, go to Canada, everything's fine in Canada, they said, everybody's rich in Canada. My arse they are."

He paused to strike several useless matches and contemplate the perfidy of his fellow men.

Then he added: "You can sell out, Chrissake, and go orf. But I bought a little 'ouse over the 'ill there an' I'm trapped an' knackered wiv a wife an' all. Now look at me."

Looking, I beheld a man not above five feet in height, stooped and skeletal. His eyes, like the eyes of a cooked mackerel, protruded from a narrow wedge of pallid face, and his teeth, fashioned by an unskilled dentist, seemed to oscillate at random. To me, Snape would always remain a fixed portrait of despair, even when he entertained the neighbours with a homemade potation vaguely resembling beer. As the bottles were opened, most of the contents exploded into the kitchen sink, a fraction into the guests.

But these occasions came later. At our first meeting he was anxious to recall his career in the British Army. He had been a batman to some officer, and his service had taken him to India.

"Orful country, Injia," he said. "Full of snakes and dead corpses on the streets, smellin' bad. An' the rajas. . . ."

He paused again, evidently wondering if he should give me some secret but essential data and groping for a chaste description of Indian society lest he offend my innocent Canadian ears.

Then, in the crisp official idiom of a private soldier reporting to his colonel: "All the rajas kept a lot of fat young boys for purposes of private buggery."

My ears were not offended, but I paid no attention to Snape's warning against the country life. At the age of twenty-three, planning to marry next year, and not yet the neighbourhood's crank nor a killer with weapons more efficient and poisons more deadly than any known to the Borgias of Italy, I had everything to learn.

When no houses were in sight and the town stood four miles away on a winding gravel road, how could I imagine a siege of subdivisions, a four-lane highway, a clatter of traffic, a buzz of planes and helicopters, the advance of civilization and progress? That the pond at the bottom of the hill would be drained and covered with bungalows, that we would no longer hear the frog chorus in February or that the pheasants, quail and mallards would depart even before Snape, did not occur to me.

So far, I hadn't asked myself why, on sudden impulse, I wanted to live in the country. Much less did I foresee a second life in the wilderness of Vancouver Island and a third, negligent life as a newspaperman. I was afflicted with triple schizophrenia. Least of all did I suspect the joint creaturehood around me, the total interdependence of living things—from the bacteria to the human species. The most important of lessons was to take more than half a century, and it is far from complete near the end.

Still, I was beginning to understand, dimly, that humans divorced from nature lose their vital juices, that the apparatus of society, like my own pastoral fantasy, disguised the real facts of life too grim for direct vision.

More knowledge of them awaited more experience, but already the mossy rocks of my brief lifetime lease informed me that they had been rounded and polished only yesterday, as planetary time is reckoned, and the glaciers would return tomorrow. Man's precarious freehold on the earth was writ large across the countryside.

After studying nature's alphabet for a decade or two I learned to read a little of it. In a drop of rain water hanging from a twig and reflecting a minute cosmos when the sun came out again, in summer blossom and winter tempest, in the eyes of a child at play or the grin of an old dog, wisps and flickers of reality were sometimes visible.

Plato's fable of humanity imprisoned where it could see nothing but the shadows of real substance moving outside the cave told the truth of things long ago. It needed no elaboration by modern prisoners like me. Besides, as G. K. Chesterton once remarked, "It is only a rare and amazing miracle when a man really says what he means."

Up to now I have never achieved that miracle.

In my first newspaper days I made two unlikely intimates, twice my age, and both of them confirmed Harry Snape's advice.

Percy Rawling was a chunky, square-faced native of England, a fellow reporter in the Victoria police court, a jack of many trades, with blunt speech, total honesty and eccentric habits. He always carried several pipes in his bulging pockets, travelled in a cloud of fragrant English tobacco smoke, owned seven danger- ous, old-fashioned razors (one for each day of the week), scorned the safe modern types as effeminate and regularly nicked his cheeks.

Rawling had farmed in Manitoba, sailed before the mast on the Pacific, worked in the mines of Colorado, covered labour wars and bombings for the rowdy Denver *Post* and, far past mil- itary age, joined the Canadian army of the First World War. Refusing a commission, he fought in Europe with the rank of corporal until the German gas attack at Ypres seared his lungs and almost killed him. He was moved to the milder climate of Palestine where, using his miner's skills, he helped to dynamite Turkish bridges for Lawrence of Arabia.

The gas at Ypres left him wheezing, gurgling and painfully struggling for speech. He had, in addition, some verbal oddities not quite cockney though close to it. Often he would open a sentence with "yem, yem" instead of "yes" and finish it, if angry, with "gar, gar." These mutterings, we supposed, were relics of boyhood in the London home of a prosperous cloth merchant, who used to jump on his silk hat or hurl food against the dining room wall to emphasize some point of domestic argument.

"My poor child," said Percy when I told him of my land pur- chase, "you're not cut out for it, you're stark mad. The thing won't work. You a farmer? God almighty, you're not even a newspaperman yet."

His cheeks broke into baby dimples as he meditated one of his bizarre conceits. "Yem, yem, the trouble is, you haven't drunk enough and slept in the gutter. Too bad, but I never force good liquor on the young if the supply is limited. Gar, you seriously mean to spend your life with broken shovels and potted rhododendrons?"

While I owned none of these articles, he was so pleased with his imagery that he wrote it, and me, with reckless embellishment, into a newspaper column and predicted that I would soon return to the city.

My folly seemed even more alarming to Benny Nicholas, a second bachelor and the entirely bald, spherical and legendary editor of the Victoria *Daily Times*. There I had my first job, and he, the monarch of a ramshackle make-believe kingdom, alternated between screaming tantrums, prodigal undeserved charities and snatches of opera in a mellow tenor. Long before his rightful span, he was to drop dead at his typewriter.

Like Percy, he had warned me, from the start, against my rustic illusions. Glaring at the oak trees and ignoring the carpet of white native lilies beneath them, he declared that the whole neighbourhood was shady, damp and unwholesome. He sniffed the clean air, pungent with earth's incense, and said it must be dangerously infected by the surrounding dairy farms. And how could I possibly live four miles away from the office and my duties? Then he looked across the valley to the blue Sooke Hills and added: "Why, it's *unnatural*."

Percy and Benny, faithful friends, thought they understood me, but they didn't.

In spite of their warnings, I completed the fence after months of toil and hired a gloomy plowman with a tombstone visage and his asthmatic mare, at wages of forty cents an hour, to break the sod for a vegetable garden. I also hired a squat, grizzled little man with a single eye and a rawhide face half hidden by a trailing, yellow-stained moustache to dig a hole fifty feet long, thirty-five feet wide and eight feet deep for the cellar of a house.

Dick (the only name he ever mentioned) had been a hard-rock miner in Wales, Idaho and other places. He lived alone in a neat shack down the road, and now, eighty-three years of age, he undertook the massive job of excavation as a routine chore. His tools were a shovel, a pick and a wooden wheelbarrow; his fee, fifty dollars, plus half a dozen sticks of dynamite to blow up a huge oak stump. All day he never stopped digging, chewing tobacco without expectoration and apparently enjoying his work while regretting his premature celibacy.

One morning he assured me, with a mixture of pride and sorrow, "Last night I wanted the loins of a woman mighty bad, but they don't come my ways no more."

This lack could not impede his labour. In less than a month he had removed tons of earth in his wheelbarrow, blasted the stump, received his fee and avoided sobriety for several glorious days.

Two carpenters, newly arrived from Scotland and highly skilled in their trade, undertook to build the house. They mixed by hand the concrete for the massive foundation walls, selected the lumber, haggling over its price, fashioned all the cupboards and bookcases to save the cost of mill work and finished the whole job in three months.

Their wages, to their full satisfaction, were fixed at seven dollars a day, and we paid them fifty cents extra for bus fare. But they rode bicycles six miles across town every morning and every evening. Later, when they twice extended the house, their wages increased to eight dollars. Nowadays, few houses are as well built with power tools. The total cost was about ten thousand dollars for eight rooms and two bathrooms.

We had been in possession only a month or two when, alone one evening, I burned some scraps of wood left by the carpenters and started a magnificent roaring chimney fire. Flames mounted far above the roofs. Sparks flew still higher. My free pyrotechnical show must have titillated spectators for miles around.

I dashed outdoors, raised a ladder, climbed up with a garden hose, aimed the water vertically and drenched myself. These efforts had little effect, but soon the fire died without human assistance. Then Snape arrived, panting and gibbering, to explain at length that in a dry season I should burn coal, never wood.

Alas, Dick was not as fortunate as the carpenters. The swallowed nicotine and enforced abstinence from sex ruined his health, killing him in the old folks' home at the age of ninety-four.

Until those last years he had continued to accept back-breaking work, the tools light in his hands, while I discovered, by middle age, that each season the manufacturers, all of them sadists, made their shovels heavier, their saws duller and their bottled goods weaker.

Many seasons of experiment, trial, error, laughter and tears passed before I lost my youthful chimera, my friends and two irreplaceable companions. Even then I did not leave the country. Spring's bloom and green explosion, summer's tick and crackle in the forest, autumn's gilded pageant, the rumble and moan of winter gale—these sounds, moods and scents of Canada kept me earthbound.

Never a serious student of nature—or of anything else—I judged at least that humanity may be roughly divided between two estates: the people of the indoors and those of the outdoors, of street and of trail. Sometimes the twain meet in business, politics or society, but they do not speak the same inner language. Except for trivial communication, they inhabit different worlds.

My world was subject to pretty drastic change with the year's four seasons.

SPRING

The Seed
and the
Mystery

SPRING'S FIRST GARDEN, like love's first embrace, is momentous in the course of human events. But a garden lasts longer. Recharged with additional nutriment year after year, it will serve the needs of a lifetime.

Concerning this truth and many others my bride and I were totally ignorant when we began our exploration of the chilly March soil and its teeming inhabitants. At least we knew that spring on the narrow Pacific shelf was not the spring of Canada. Here, with the people of England, we drift slowly, softly, half-consciously between winter and summer. A hundred miles from the coast the seasons change in a convulsion like mammalian birth.

Suddenly the frozen rind of water and earth is broken. Inert matter writhes in mimic life. Ice tumbles and rumbles on the great rivers. White chunks, huge marshmallows, ride up and down the St. Lawrence tide past Quebec and flounder through the Hell's Gate of the Fraser.

In the high Rockies, beads of moisture ooze from a sunlit crag, every trickle finds its way into the skein of milky glacial brooklets that soon become foaming torrents carrying their freight of earth specks to three oceans. On a warming cliff, the crusted snow pack melts. An avalanche plunges to the valley and leaves a tangle of uprooted trees and a clean swath of bare rock.

Overnight, as if washed by some artist's brush of water-colour, the rounded foothills turn pale green when the bunch-grass sprouts. Willows, poplars and tamaracks, naked at dawn, wear coats of the same transparent hue at sunset.

I had known the instant Canadian spring in Ontario and Quebec, on the ranges of the Cariboo, and the Alberta prairies. Most vivid among my memories is spring in a squalid British Columbia cattle town where three small boys witnessed the turn of the year's hinge. The sleigh bells fell silent, wheels clattered again on the thawing street, and the air brought a first hint of warmth. Those boys felt, as no man can feel, the current of spring pulsing through their veins, and its call could not be resisted.

So they played hooky from school, walked a mile along the railway track, lighted a fire at the edge of the snow, boiled tea and discussed the prospects of summer and trout fishing. Then, in a distant field, they saw a colt emerge from its mother and drop to the ground. She licked the slimy covering from her baby, and the colt wobbled to its feet.

The boys had enough sense not to approach it. Farther up the track they found the body of a steer disembowelled by a passing locomotive. In one day they had beheld the wonders of spring, birth and death. Nobody spoke on the way home.

On the western seashore, as I grew older, spring offered a different spectacle. It ambled in from the sea at leisurely gait with the Japan Current, spread its salty flavour abroad with a fragrant whiff of earth and blossom.

Flabby coastal dwellers like Dot and me had watched our jasmine bush flaunt a constellation of yellow stars before the old year's end. Next came the white bells of snowdrops, apparently too weak for stormy weather yet strong enough to break through a black-topped garden path and breed colonies under the Gothic arches and intricate groining of the oak trees.

Swarms of azure crocus followed, their petals closing tight whenever a cloud hid the sun. A golden sibling bloomed a week or so later to provide a treasure trove of bullion for the honey bees.

Purple heather had been in flower since Christmas, and by mid-February rhubarb, bold pioneer of the vegetable family, thrust up its crimson buds and wrinkled leaves in a pattern of green lace. Already we had discovered the first dandelion, like a miniature chrysanthemum, its beauty rejected only because its seeds blew too far and fast on tiny parachutes and its presence was too common.

In those days the world was at peace. We were, too, but heedless of our blessings when we knelt in the gardener's posture of reverence to plant an edible crop. For this purpose we long had the help of a dairy farmer who, every year, gave us a Christmas present of rich barnyard stuff. As we scattered it thriftily on the vegetable patch, our seasoned nostrils relished the perfumes of Arabia. Nowadays, few gardeners and fewer vegetables enjoy that noisome luxury.

The worms seemed to enjoy it with special gusto, becoming fat and sleek as they continued their immemorial task. Since civilization began, or even before, in the age of food gatherers, the worm has been one of mankind's most valuable and least appreciated servants. If its myriads failed to break up the clotted earth and, by its simple digestive system, renew the planet's fertility, humans would starve. And so would other species.

In boyhood I had impaled worms on my fish hook with no thought of their value. As a countryman I scrupulously preserved them and rescued any that got lost on the paths, returning them to their natural habitation.

It was good for Dot and me to feel the loam in our hands, to plant seeds and participate, however marginally and clumsily, in the rite of creation. We grew enough vegetables to feed at least three families, and though we resolved each spring to plant less, we usually expanded the garden. There was a strange fascination in vegetables, which, unlike shrubs and trees, completed their life cycle in half a year. We didn't need to wait long to see nature's whole performance and the results of our work.

Even Harry Snape cheered up a little in the spring. The

neighbourhood's iconoclast actually encouraged us. "But yer plantin' too deep, same as me," he said, "till I caught the 'ang of it. A bunch of narsty turnips and beans, that's all. Then I planted shaller and everythink grew fine. Yer should see me onions. Lovely. Sweet as a nut."

So his onions may have been, but they led to a grave household crisis.

Next week he appeared in a state of panic.

"Tulips!" he shouted. "Are tulips pyzonous?"

"You've eaten tulips?" said Dot.

"Yus, the bulbs. Chrissake, the bulbs an' we're pyzened."

From his sputtering account we understood that Mrs. Snape, whose eyesight was defective, found some of last year's forgotten bulbs in the cellar. She cooked them as onions and served them with a sauce richly flavoured by curry and other Indian spices not easy to digest.

"They went down good," Snape told us. "But pretty quick we got bellyache, tearin' bellyache. Must be pyzonous."

I offered to drive him to the hospital in town. No use, he groaned. It was too late. No doubt the bulbs were fatal. With the stoic discipline of an old soldier, he rolled a wet and bulging cigarette. It could not be kept burning, but presently he allowed that his pain had eased. After consuming bicarbonate of soda and four glasses of sherry in our house, he went back to his own, pausing to shout, "Plant shaller!"

Mrs. Snape, we subsequently learned, also survived after he lectured her on the fine points of agronomy and the high cost of tulip bulbs.

Meanwhile we accepted his advice and planted closer to the surface. The rate of seed germination certainly improved. But we were still too young for serious contemplation of seeds as the humble allegory of mankind's life. For every human being originated in a seed. All we knew at the beginning was that a few dollars bought seeds enough to produce more food than our household could eat. In future seasons we discovered that planting was no guarantee of reaping. Vigorous seedlings often became the defenceless prey of insects, disease spores or roaming rabbits.

Such casualties were not the fault of the seeds. Only in middle age, however, did I begin to see what a mystery was locked in a pellet smaller than the head of a match.

Throughout the ages, men of genius have built cities, written books, composed music, and invented weapons that can now end planetary life. They have cross-fertilized the pollen of flowers to develop new plant varieties, but they have never unlocked the secret of growth. With all its wizardry and machines, science has changed nothing in the essential nature of the seed and devised no alternative. Only seeds can produce other seeds and nourish life much larger than their own. Every seed is a fragment of immortality.

How strange, how frightening when you think about it, is the limited scope of human power, so masterful, so educated and wise yet so dependent on a few inches of topsoil, which erosion is carrying away and man-made chemicals are polluting. Inside this shrinking layer, multitudinous organisms, visible only through a microscope, quicken at spring's alert with a collective force stronger than any nuclear bomb. If their innocent explosion failed, even for a year, civilization would need no bomb to destroy it.

The public seldom gives thought to such decisive facts, instead concentrating on relatively minor concerns like politics, business, crime or scandal. Mankind's pursuit of red herrings is always enthusiastic, often absurd. Thus, for instance, we in Canada debate with comic alarm our national identity, asking whether it really exists, though it was never in doubt since that spring long ago when Champlain had outlived a winter of scurvy and starvation and "out of the twenty-eight first forming our company only eight remained and half of them ailing."

The breed to be identified as Canadian had arrived. Thenceforth, like all breeds, it would change its habits and viewpoint, but its character, in wisdom or in folly, would remain distinct. So would the identity of the seed as the custodian of the universal life-dynamism older by countless aeons than humanity.

If this be cliché, I needed many years in garden and forest to recognize its meaning and to understand that the obvious, though generally suspect nowadays, is generally true, one of the

most neglected truths as a man takes his companions and comforts for granted until they disappear.

Yes, cliché, but a folk memory or earth instinct surely recurs
among men and women of the Northern Hemisphere soon after
the December solstice. When the planet turns on its axis, just as
surely the day's junk mail brings the annual seed temptation.
The catalogues are full of gaudy deceit, of pictured vegetables
and blooms never seen in any garden hereabouts. But hopefully
assuming that reach must exceed grasp or what's a garden for,
we buy the unfamiliar varieties of seed and usually find their
products less satisfactory than the familiar ones.

Now, every garden and hardware shop is crowded with ardent amateurs who buy more shovels, hoes, rakes, hoses, sprays
and fertilizers than they will need in a normal lifetime. Among
the dilettantes, this spasm will barely outlast the first days of
May. Only the true believers, as distinguished from the triflers,
stay the course to harvest season. Most of the vernal nature
lovers are soon playing golf or politics, sailing boats or travelling abroad, and their plants wither from drought. All societies
have their privileged classes that neither plant nor reap but expect others to feed them.

Such notions did not interrupt our planting. When Percy
Rawling arrived one day (bringing his invariable beefsteak two
inches thick and a flask of rum for his exclusive use) he found us
thinning a row of carrots. He stood a while watching our
slaughter and catching his breath after the walk down the lane
from the bus.

"You mean to say you like this kind of thing?" he grumbled
at last. "It's masochism, but you never heard the word. And the
stuff may grow even for you young devils."

"And why wouldn't it?" said Dot.

"Right me darlin' hell cat. Yem, yem, why not? Growth, it's
a mystery. I admit it."

"You admit the mystery? Well, well. That's big of you, very
big."

So it was in a belligerent agnostic.

His baby dimples appeared. "Cease and desist, young devils.
I've no wind to argue. You might as well ask the meaning of the

universe and it makes no sense to me. But the steak! Ha, it needs cookin' and I need a rum ration and if you don't treat me better I'll take them back to town, by God, and you can keep the carrots and the universe."

His point seemed valid. We adjourned to our kitchen for dinner.

Our second friend and benefactor, Benny Nicholas, avoided the outdoors as much as possible, but he had a generous heart and was no agnostic, though he went to church only for weddings and funerals. He also had, we guessed, a kind of laughing, jeering, shouting reverence for some mystical truth never defined.

About this time a sickly little man called at the editor's messy office and said he was Jesus, newly risen. To prove his claim, he showed the scars of crucifixion on his hands.

Benny did not question the stranger's tale. Instead, he sent him to the leading Christian minister of the town for spiritual communion. An hour later the preacher telephoned to accuse Benny of flagrant sacrilege.

"Nicholas," he protested, "you've sent me a lunatic who says he's our Saviour!"

"And how," Benny demanded, "would you know he isn't? The last time Jesus came, you churchmen nailed him to a cross."

In church, garden, everywhere, the mystery endured, and now for us it was expanding into new territory and even more primitive ways of life.

The Bridge
to Solitude

NEAR THE OCEAN'S THERMOSTAT spring comes early. A few miles away, in the virgin forest, it comes late to expose winter's havoc. Here we found no token of life, no animals, birds or insects, no whisper of wind or creak of branch. For reasons unknown the weather seemed to pause, the silence broken only by the faint lisp of water in tiny runnels and the brimming sponge underfoot.

A coastal forest needs no sound to advertise the spring's business, no gabble of television, no hourly flashes of news from the sweet security of streets where most Canadians feel at home. But for those of us more uncouth and less attuned to the march of civilization, the silent wilderness is not depressing or even dumb. By its own methods it communicates with the seasoned ear, or at least with human imagination.

Its message is simple, clear as print, and hostile—trespassers are unwelcome. The sunny deciduous woods of central Canada invite man to their open corridors. In the tangled underbrush, matted salal, spiked devil's club, sodden floor and brooding dark of the western coast, man is an enemy to be intimidated and repulsed.

Thus warned, city drivers seldom venture from the main roads before summer. They do not see how wind, frost and deep snowfall have levelled the trees in haphazard patches like the work of a blind reaper with his scythe. Some of the firs and cedars, centuries old and massive of diameter, looked healthy and invincible last autumn. Now they lay prostrate, their huge trunks shattered. In the wilderness, as in human life, the giants often died too soon while the dwarfs and weaklings were spared by nature's caprice.

What savage gales must have roared through the winter jungle, what screech of tearing heartwood, what crash and thud when the giants fell and no man heard them die!

If man does not intrude, nature will repair all the damage. In fact, repairs never cease. Throughout the year the roots spread and ramify in search of moisture and nourishment. The unseen competition of this free market is more ruthless and more efficient than man's fumbling economy.

Space surrendered by winter's victims will be quickly occupied by their successors. Extra sunlight will breed a new generation. Already, before their evergreen competitors, alders have taken advantage of their good luck to increase their kind. Pendulous catkins, dyed in Burgundy, will become seeds for next year's growth. Maple buds begin to swell and feel sticky. Sword ferns prepare to unwind their tight coils, and skunk cabbage to wave yellow banners of defiance with a bracing scent. Soon the hoarse love song of the frogs will rise from the swamp, the slugs will appear in shiny green uniforms, and the arrow flight of clamorous geese, bound north, will print its ancient calligraphy upon the sky.

But not yet. For true spring we must wait several more weeks. In the meantime we performed a ritual that no city dweller could understand.

At the end of a winding trail half a mile long and on the far side of a little gully crossed by a rotting footbridge stood a cabin. Inherited from Dot's parents, it was a poor sort of cabin, a botched job of nameless carpenters long ago, a lopsided shell of boards that lacked the solid dignity of logs and seemed likely to collapse at any moment into the gully behind it or the lake in front. Its walls were flimsy and crooked, its roof leaky, its underpinnings decayed. But, rebuilt and expanded, this rickety structure became, until death parted us, the centre of our joint life, then the lives of our children, grandchildren and great-grandchildren.

Year after year, the spring ritual never changed. We found the key, secreted under the bridge where the most incompetent burglar would be sure to find it, and pushed open the warped back door. An icy draft, accumulated all winter, struck us like a fist.

In a kitchen with a single window and dark on a day of sunshine, we lighted a coal-oil lamp and soon had a fire burning in the rusty stove. Now we surveyed the winter's negligible indoor damage.

If any burglar had entered, he had seen nothing worth stealing. Rats had munched a cake of soap carelessly left on the table. Mice had deposited their calling cards of thanks for meals of spilled flour. A squirrel that hibernated above the ceiling had dropped some of his pine cones onto the floor. The roof had usually leaked in only a couple of places—inevitably upon the beds.

It would take us many hours, and exertions about as strenuous as a four-minute mile or the ascent of a high mountain, to carry the mattresses outside and dry them on the clothesline, to mop the floors, fix the leaks with roof gum and prop up the sagging bridge. It was many years before we had saved enough money to rebuild the cabin and equip it with big windows, electricity, plumbing and comfortable furniture.

Our guests approved these luxuries and perhaps they flattered our house pride. But we were never to be so happy again as in those primitive days when we carried all supplies on our backs half a mile from the road, and water in pails from the lake and bathed in a tin washtub before the weather warmed for swimming. Nobody, I suppose, appreciates the animal zest of youth until it has fled.

That loss was a decade or two ahead of us. For the time being the cabin, however shabby and disreputable, seemed to possess a life of its own, as if it had pined for human company since last fall and now rejoiced in our appearance. Its lining of brown-stained cedar boards was impregnated with memories of men, women and children long departed, their voices still audible in our private ears. No stranger could share these fantasies, and I did not expect that some other beloved voices, then heard as physical sounds, would soon be heard no more.

In the meantime, why did we come here, leaving a modern house and a pleasant garden? The reason, no doubt, was empty figment, the pretence of hardy pioneer life when we were not brave or foolish enough to face it in reality. Here we could escape, at least, the ring of telephones, the world's news and the routine of my trade. An hour's drive from the city, we were still conditioned by it, but our little plot of wilderness was unspoiled, its life untouched, so far, by progress.

When, later, we travelled all over Europe, we saw that the Old World, even beyond the cities, was smoothed, coddled and truly civilized as the New World was not. But, returning home, we rejoiced in Canada's wild hinterland and knew that our people, with all their riches, were neither as sophisticated, disillusioned or cynical as the Europeans.

A history much wider than the Atlantic divides two continents. No one understands the division without travelling both. And no one ever *owns* a cabin or an acre of forest, whatever the title deeds in the land registry may say. We were transient tenants to be quickly forgotten like our predecessors, Indian and white. But the forest lived on, perpetually renewing itself, and the cabin, with annual repairs, would easily last another century.

Not yet fully aware of these facts, we found our immediate necessities daunting. First we had to build a new bridge eighty feet long over a gully fifteen feet deep. The old one was the work of a lazy builder who had used young fir trees about three inches thick to support it and hadn't bothered to skin them. Of course they immediately began to rot, and now the whole bridge was a public menace.

Since I had never built anything larger than a dog kennel (which our dog refused to enter), I consulted Percy Rawling, whose numerous careers included carpentry and fine cabinet making. He followed us along the trail and observed our deathtrap bridge in panting silence.

13

Then, catching his breath, he croaked, "God almighty, whoever did this thing should be hanged, drawn and quartered so he can't do it again. Gar, knock it down, knock it down before it kills somebody."

This was impractical advice when we needed to cross the gully a dozen times every day. So Percy followed us on the shaky span, taking care not to touch the broken handrails, and we installed him by the kitchen stove with his rum ration.

After a third glass and mature thought, he explained in detail how we could erect a new bridge. Warming to the subject and recalling his days of dynamiting Turkish bridges with Lawrence of Arabia, he said, "You don't know anything about the principles of construction, the laws of stress and gravity. Yem, yem, listen to me, young devils. When they built the cathedrals of England they'd ornament construction but never construct ornament. Don't forget that law, ever."

"It's not a cathedral," Dot protested. "It's only a little wooden bridge!"

"No matter," said Percy. "The principle is the same. Those old builders knew what they were doing."

"And suppose they did," said Dot. "What of it?"

"Ha, the janglin' and jonglin' of this monstrous regiment of women!"

And with sublime irrelevance he added, "Remember, me darlin', kind hearts are more than coronets, and simple faith than Norman blood."

We never knew what unlikely specimens Percy would discover in the book-filled attic of his mind.

Despite his warnings, the old bridge, with some new props, lasted another year while I pondered its replacement. For such a massive undertaking I lacked Percy's skill in woodcraft. A spacious armchair and a splendid refectory table of oak, still in the cabin, are the work of his hands. Many faded clippings of his newspaper column remind us of his wordcraft and, more important, the qualities of his indestructible English breed.

All the ponderous jokes and wheezing chuckles of this gallant man did not fool us as we grew in age and perhaps in understanding. For reasons never disclosed to us, he was, after a lifetime of varied trades and adventures, a sad and solitary man, the victim, we guessed, of some secret misfortune before the gas attack at Ypres. No one could fill the gap of his departure.

From time to time other gaps opened in our lives as in the forest. F. A. McDiarmid, Dot's father, a short, sturdy man learned in the law and human nature, had bought the cabin and a narrow lakefront property during an illness because his doctors had prescribed the healing outdoors. Later on, we greatly expanded his purchase.

He spent much time playing solitaire under a gasoline lamp while meditating his cases in the Vancouver courts. Or he would row a flat-bottomed punt, trolling a spoon and even, occasionally, catching a trout. But a cedar-strip canoe was his real treasure, the only camp possession he seemed to value. As an expert trained on the stormy lakes of northern Ontario, he taught me how to paddle with minimum stress. That skill was rare on our lake. After his time I, too, valued his frail yet lovely craft until a fat girl jumped into it and broke a dozen ribs—not hers, regrettably.

F. A. was a man of superior mind and kindly disposition but handless. The bridge and the cabin might have tumbled down without his interference. I had just started to repair them when he died.

His wife, a woman of saintly disposition whom everyone adored and called Muzzie, took delight in cooking on her smoky stove, miraculously stretching her available groceries and feeding crowds of hungry visitors. Her simple piety and goodness almost reproduced the biblical loaves and fishes. But we were too young to appreciate her humble talent, and she asked, and expected, no thanks. For Muzzie, as for Percy, there could be no substitute.

About this time a small, thin man with a face of well-tanned leather paddled along the lake from his shack in a dilapidated canoe and offered to cut stove wood for us. I had learned in my high-school holidays the use of a six-foot cross-cut saw at wages of a dollar a cord, but now I lacked time to deal with all the trees felled by winter storm. So I employed the paddler and saw at once that he was a true creature of the wilderness.

The muscles on his short figure were far stronger than mine. He would string a rope from the end of his saw to a convenient sapling, which, bending forward and backward, eased his labour. With sledgehammer and wedge he split the rounds of wood as easily as most men cracked a walnut.

But these were his crude skills. When I could afford it, in middle age, I hired him to cut, with exquisite precision, twelve long, square, cedar beams for the living room of our rebuilt cabin. He dragged them down a mountainside behind his old flivver and towed them across the lake behind his canoe. When I asked the price he said he thought fifty dollars would not be too much. Nowadays those timbers, signed with the marks of his broadaxe, are priceless, and their like, hereabouts, is unobtainable.

Long after he had gone I celebrated his memory in a fashion that still pricks my conscience, though not too severely. Under the single name of Archie he often appeared in my newspaper columns, disguised by a white beard, a quenchless thirst for whiskey and a stubborn aversion to work of any sort. Without the least scruple I reported this sage's comments on the gossip of an imagined village and the actual politics of the nation. His outrageous heresies and mocking slanders apparently titillated the public. Some readers even supposed that he existed. And, in print, he still does.

A Lovesome
Thing,
God Wot

ALL THE POETS pried at spring, but none could distil its essence.
Like every important human experience, spring defies language.
The Oxford Dictionary of Quotations has indexed seventy-four
poetic (and prose) references to a phenomenon that antedates
language by millions of years.

The gardener lacks time for poetry, as we always found after
a carefree weekend in the woods. Although we might regret the
hasty departure of the daffodils, we did not pause, like Herrick,
for tears. Wordsworth's heart may have danced with sweet-
memoried blossom, but there is no record of his toil in any garden. Browning longed for England when April and daffodils
were there, but he remained by choice under the warm sun of
Italy.

For poets, golfers and triflers of all sorts, spring is a time of
freedom and leisure. For us it had become a stern master.

We had plenty of daffodils, hundreds of them bought at bar-
gain prices from a commercial grower and carelessly thrust into
the sod beneath the oaks. A gift of violet roots was installed
nearby and forgotten until, three seasons later, we beheld a con-
gregation of tiny purple faces, each with an orange nose and
neat black whiskers.

The native flora was even more prolific. Lilies (as they were called hereabouts when their real and ugly name was Erythronium) thrust up their brown-dappled leaves, then their white flowers, and snow seemed to be drifting in April. Beside them arose their pink cousins, wearing upturned petals that looked like Indian war-bonnets. They were followed by the lofty blue spikes of camass, whose bulbs were a staple of the Indians' diet.

When all these plants brought a silent music to the gardener's ear, we ventured to rephrase Shakespeare's famous line—the man who had no blossom in himself was fit for treasons, stratagems and spoils. Let no such man be trusted.

Observing the host of daffodils and listening in fancy to the peal of their brave little trumpets, we had yet to hear of a vicious fly, their destroyer. After a few years it discovered and systematically looted our treasures. Its eggs hatched a grub that descended into the earth and feasted on the bulb's core, the embryo of the flower. Every spring more and more daffodil stalks lived flowerless and blind. Fiercer enemies had yet to arrive.

Now that April, much like England's season, was here, the seedlings of carrots, spinach, beets and lettuce marched in crowded rows and had to be mercilessly thinned. All our spare time was needed to pamper the vegetables, but it was pleasant work.

Across the lane, the farmer strode behind his giant Clydesdales and his plow while screaming gulls fought each other for worms in the upturned earth. One of his unknown predecessors had long ago planted on land now ours a grove of plum trees. The two survivors bloomed lavishly still and in autumn produced more prunes than we and our friends could use, even though Harry Snape converted some of the fruit into a nauseating, sickly-sweet cordial.

Spring had reached its climax when Percy Rawling found us, as usual, on our knees in the vegetable patch. After several hours of weeding we were cramped, cranky and in no mood for Percy's ponderous wit (though we welcomed his traditional beefsteak). He grinned down at us without offering any comment on our task.

"If you've come to gloat," said Dot, "go away, just go away."

"Hold your peace, hellcat," Percy wheezed. Then, dimpling, he conceived a feeble pun on a famous line of poetry. "A garden is a loathsome thing, God wot."

The hellcat glared up at him. "And so are you, God wot."

Percy winked at me. "Poor soul, but she's just as happy as if she had good sense."

The insatiable reader of ancient books dragged out of thin air an unlikely quotation. "Yem, yem, we carry within us the wonders we seek without us: there is all Africa and her prodigies in us."

That could be so, but at the moment there was in us only a keen hunger. So Percy's steak was cooked and we nibbled our earliest radishes, the true, incarnadined heralds of spring.

Our energies were not confined to vegetables. We encircled the house with rhododendrons, azalias, camelias, forsythias and other shrubs bought at a price we could not afford. But they grew swiftly and paid handsome future dividends.

Our primary interest, however, was in trees. We acquired far too many of them from commercial nurseries or dug them up in the forest around our camp. As we then supposed, they would not shade us but our successors. Instead, firs, cedars, spruce and a California redwood, mere twigs when we planted them, are now almost four feet in diameter at their base. These conifers, unlike their fellows of the wild, lived in open space without competition for light. As a result, the lower branches did not die and fall off but, thriving, gave the trees a symmetrical contour as if a sculptor had moulded them.

We also moved young dogwoods from the forest and waited half a dozen years for their first elegant white blossoms, whose seeds took root in unexpected places. We even managed to transplant a few arbutus saplings with roots two feet long, but the casualty rate was high.

After a decade we were surrounded, and in cloudy weather sometimes even felt threatened by a minor jungle. But on a sunny April day the changing landscape exceeded our hopes. The blossom of Japanese plums and cherries frothed against the evergreens. The blue skyline of the Sooke Hills was pierced by the hundred-foot exclamation marks of our lombardy poplars.

Scents too mixed and subtle for analysis filled the air, none so bittersweet to old folk with youthful memories as the lilac's squandered redolence. "When lilacs last in the dooryard bloomed" is perhaps the most poignant line in American literature, and for us they bloomed faithfully year after year, despite our neglect.

With amateur's luck my plantings succeeded, in some places, too well. Birds dispersed the seeds of holly, broom, wild cherry, red osier and even dogwood until I was forced to attack unwanted copses. But my axe, machete and muscles could never subdue the blackberry vines that had escaped from gardens unknown and made some thickets impenetrable.

When, for a single family, I planted an orchard of about thirty fruit trees—apples, pears, plums, cherries and even peaches, whose blooms usually froze—my ignorance (or greed) betrayed me. I did not foresee the work of pruning, spraying and picking. Worse, I knew nothing of our devastating enemy's transcontinental advance.

Already an incurable disease had killed our raspberries. Earwigs nibbled the perennials. Weevils devoured the roots of strawberries and primroses. But so far, no gardener west of the Maritimes had encountered the winter moth, so named because it laid its eggs not long before Christmas. I was in middle age when some of the eggs were carried across the country to Vancouver Island, though not to the mainland and Vancouver.

In the first visible omen of disaster, clouds of small brown moths fluttered against our windows. Next spring the blooms of the orchard failed to produce any fruit. Skilled entomologists did not recognize the invader, and my ebbing strength was quickly exhausted in vain attempts to halt a ravening march of green caterpillars, each about the size of a pin's head. They multiplied and guzzled at a terrifying rate and could strip a large tree bare in half a day.

By this time I was a fairly competent poisoner. Since my early days I had used lime and sulphur spray, when the trees were dormant, to nullify the eggs of the comparatively harmless tent caterpillars. But my first experiment was calamitous.

Since I had not worn a mask or gloves, I was painfully burned and remained dormant, under a doctor's care, for three weeks. And even after I took reasonable precautions my presence seemed unwelcome indoors, for I reeked of spray. It was said that I wafted a strong aroma of rotten eggs.

In those days lethal substances were used without restriction or any sense of danger. Not until recent years did humanity begin to understand that it was poisoning the rivers, the lakes, the atmosphere and itself. Even now the process of gradual suicide continues on a changed but larger scale, and we are informed by respected economists that the fluids and fumes of industry must be accepted to keep our living standard rising (as if consumption alone measures the pursuit of happiness).

The current environmental debate was in its preliminary phase when I grappled with the caterpillar invasion, and all the precautions recommended by the experts failed. It had been thought that a band of vile sticky stuff around the trunk of each tree would trap the enemies as they hatched and ascended from the earth. Some caterpillars were trapped, but after several years of fruitless trees it was discovered that the wrong insect had perished. The cunning winter moth laid its eggs on the branches, not the earth. Its progeny could be repelled only by poison.

So, in the merry month of May began my springtime of horror, despair and longing for the hibernal comforts of wintry cold. Once the fruit buds turned pink the season of misery could be delayed no longer. At dawn, because only then was the air still, I would climb a high, shaky ladder, garbed like an astronaut, my torso protected by a waterproof jumper, my legs by a stiff material known as tin pants, my hands by rubber gloves and my face by a suffocating mask. A hose extended from a bucket of spray to a brass pump, which I manipulated until my clothes were soaked and my arms aching and paralyzed.

Despite all the precautions, I must have absorbed some toxic chemicals, and assuredly my disposition was poisoned. But what worried me at the moment was the need to repeat the spray treatment after the blossoms fell. That I didn't fall, too, from the shaky ladder was surprising, and in the nick of time came relief.

Having identified the guilty species, the entomologists imported predatory bees to feed on the caterpillars, and their population gradually declined. After six barren years I managed to produce a plentiful crop, and the neighbouring boys reaped it with diligent efficiency, leaving us no samples from the young trees now bearing their first fruits.

By such minor losses I learned that a garden or an orchard, like a marriage, should not be undertaken lightly or unadvisedly and that on the land, as in society, there is no justice. The country man seems to work most of his time not with but against Mother Nature. She is threatened by human folly all over the planet, but in our tiny patch she always defeated us, unjustly as we supposed, not knowing her purposes.

Thus soft, inexperienced migrants from the city often grew vegetables and flowers far better than mine. With all my labour and study of garden books I could not make some common plants happy. Aubretia, alyssum and primroses throve in the gardens of raw novices but sulked and moped in ours. After many disappointments I realized that I could not become a real gardener. My hands lacked the necessary cunning, my disposition was too impatient, my methods too hasty.

The only real gardener I knew was my father, who had imported and successfully grown in his little Victoria garden the seeds of exotic rock plants from the mountains of Switzerland, India and the United States. He came to live with us and established a plant nursery on the open meadow land. Its profits paid his full share of our capital and running costs, while my mother, a superb cook, helped Dot in the kitchen.

Hutch, as everybody called my father, saw the opportunity of a lifetime in the bare rocks surrounding and overtopping the house. Together, he and I carried in baskets tons of earth to fill the crevices, and heavy stones to build retaining walls. Soon, in beds of fertile mould, his exotics covered the rocks with greenery and bloom.

When alone with them he constantly talked to his darlings as he cultivated them and doubtless believed, though he never discussed such matters, that they responded to his affection. So, indeed, they seemed to do. His faith in seed, soil and growth had become a private religion. It sustained him in comfort until the end. But it imposed stern duties.

In freezing winter nights he put on a huge, clumsy overcoat, lighted a coal-oil lantern (he distrusted electric torches and other modern gadgetry), walked a quarter of a mile on a narrow path to his greenhouse and stoked its furnace.

Cold weather was his time for building more stone walls and flower beds on the level ground. He built so many of them that our place was known as Rockhome, a name not completely forgotten in the neighbourhood even now, when I am the last survivor of the early, happy days.

Hutch's walls ignored all the conventional rules and were never scarred by cement or mortar, but they had a special quality. Unlike any others I have observed, they seemed to dance, and they are still dancing in my old age while his ashes lie where he wished, in his rockery.

After he had gone, my time, energy and talent were not enough to maintain all his green heritage. Most of the delicate rock plants disappeared in competition with vigorous brooms, heathers, cotoneasters and self-seeded dogwoods. In later years, all I could manage were the lawns, the shrubberies and the vegetable garden. But in our salad days, though we worked to no design and foresaw no results, Dot and I transformed our rural acreage and our wilderness retreat.

The Free
and the
Earthbound

ONE DAY, puttering around our wilderness cabin, we watched spring ripen to maturity as a flock of Canada geese moved north. Though they flew high, we could hear their honking, even the whisper of their wings, and read the native script legible to all Canadians, filled with gladness and wild regret.

We craned our necks to follow the flight. An old man fishing from a rowboat painfully straightened his back, shaded his eyes and gazed at the noblest of birds. Two youngsters stood up in their canoe and almost overturned it. The shouting kids on the wharf fell silent until the flock disappeared behind Mount Malahat.

Everywhere the geese were moving north, and everywhere Canadians beheld in them senses denied to mankind. Without map, compass, knowledge of geography or power of reason, the geese travel thousands of miles to their nesting grounds. They have no doubt and no fear, while humans, doubtful always, frightened always, see a creature apparently inferior to them but with a freedom and a surety that they mislaid long ago in the glut of living.

The geese know their way across the trackless land, the rivers, lakes and tundra; men stumble and fall in the pursuit of happiness. The geese fly boldly into the unknown, and it is hospitable to them; men huddle in their cities under fragile roofs to escape the stars and the terrifying void of the universe.

All Canadians look up to follow the geese wedges against the sky and feel an urgent longing in their hearts. The young are touched by a wild surmise. The old discern the swift and bitter passage of their lives. For the geese there is a certain destination and a journey that never fails, while we are bound to the earth.

The fetters binding camp denizens like Dot and me are especially tight at this season. A woodland cabin may be the most dependable retreat from a world well lost, but it demands much service and constant repair. Defying the laws of gravity, this edifice is supported by some inner principle unfamiliar to architects. Like all durable works, it is built on the foundation of a dream. Held together by invisible hoops of affection as strong as steel, it survives not only the physical climate but the mental weather of a demented age.

Before we set a temperamental hand pump close to the lake and a discarded oil drum on stilts for a tank behind the cabin, pails continued to be our waterworks. But when some twenty minutes at the long handle of our new pump lifted forty gallons to the oil drum, we felt almost too civilized.

Even when a branch road had been built years later, it was not allowed past our boundary. To the present day the cabin is reached by a quarter-mile walk. But now we are civilized enough to transport supplies on the ultimate perfection of the wheel—a light, efficient, aluminum wheelbarrow. Our whole organization, such as it is, depends on this simple and superb machine. By making a road unnecessary, it guards our seclusion, that rarest and most expensive product on today's market.

By late middle age we could no longer escape the general craze for improvements of all sorts. The cabin was totally rebuilt, but it failed to increase our happiness, only the comfort of our guests. Like a theatre audience, they did not see the months of springtime preparation and labour before the summer opening. Then, behind the producers' backs, they would criticize the play, the service, the food and drink. Or so we suspected as we distributed complimentary tickets and made ready for our modest seasonal repertoire.

These, of course, were unworthy suspicions when even solitude sometimes bored us and we were eager for company. Lacking it, camp people found plenty of time to think. The city had a superior apparatus of thought with its university, libraries, specialists of every kind and that highest source of wisdom, the television set. Although they offered grand, abstract ideas, as young folk our minds were on practical, immediate things, not culture or humanity's dubious prospects.

The imperative project, contemplated one year, procrastinated over another, its dimensions appalling, its raw materials beyond our means, was to build a new bridge. The old one seemed likely to collapse at any moment, forcing us to crawl up and down the gully.

Our friend Percy had a low and accurate opinion of my carpentry.

"You'll never build it," he said. "Never. Or if you do it won't be safe. Gar, it'll be a man trap. No, no, hire a carpenter."

For once the sage was wrong. Unable to afford a carpenter, I resolved to undertake the job myself. It required two summers, but with energy and perseverance that are now unbelievable, I built a strong bridge.

At the fringe of our property I had felled cedars about eight inches in diameter, skinned them and, using a rope, dragged timbers some twenty feet long to the gully, a quarter of a mile away. How I raised the vertical posts, braced them with temporary scaffolding, laid the horizontal beams and finally the thick planks brought from the sawmill by a steam tugboat and barge at a price of about twenty dollars per thousand board feet—all this I can no longer imagine.

Half the bridge was built in one season, half the next. It was a clumsy job, though safe enough as Percy admitted with obvious reluctance. "You'll never understand construction," he grumbled. "You'll never make a carpenter."

That was true, and to demonstrate his own remaining skill, despite his age and ruined health, he built an elaborate and finely jointed sawhorse for us. On it I cut our firewood, and after threescore years it is still in use.

But the master of construction had overlooked his own

errors. Advised by him, I mounted the bridge posts on flattened cedar logs that rotted after a dozen years. So did the cross members supporting the deck. I was compelled to build another bridge, the third on the same site and the most durable.

Luckily my two children and their friends, at minimum wages to buy candy and ice cream, helped me drag new timber out of the forest, but they were too small for bridge work and, when paid, hurried off to the village store in our rowboat.

By then I had learned something about construction and also the process of rot. Invisible armies of bacteria never paused for rest as they consumed their diet of wood. They were essential to all higher forms of life, and nothing could permanently resist their hunger, though certain precautions delayed it. I mounted the thirsty ends of the bridge posts on big flat stones, covered the beams and crosspieces with strips of tin and occasionally replaced the unprotected railings as they decayed. Lack of moisture foiled the bacteria for quite a long time.

After half a century the bridge has remained in good repair and should easily outlast its builder. Obedient to Percy's laws of construction, it bears heavy foot traffic but no ornament. Frequently repainted darkest green, it fits comfortably into the forest. Many wilderness men could have made a better bridge, and I acquired, very late, a decent respect for their humble talents.

While I laboured on my first bridge in the early days, spring was advancing fast towards summer and the woods had donned their new finery. The native currant bushes wore garnet earrings and exhaled astringent perfume. Skunk cabbages flourished yellow chalices, violets of similar hue bloomed at the edge of the swamp, white trilliums dappled the forest floor, bleeding hearts dropped pink tears, Indian paintbrush was tipped with vivid gules, sword ferns and bracken unwound their coils, the buds of maple alder burst their winter rinds.

A mixed fragrance alerted our nostrils, the resinous emanation of the conifers, the sweet whiff of wild roses and honeysuckle, the clean, brave smell of warming earth and naked rock.

Now the spring silence was broken. A gentle breeze murmured through evergreen needles. The frog orchestra sounded a crescendo in the swamp. Willow grouse drummed their love message, squirrels chattered in the trees, the parliament of ravens began its hoarse annual debate, the shrill voice of the kingfisher and the haunting cry of the loon rose from the lake, and high above it eagles soared and mewed.

When ugly human sounds disrupted nature's harmony— speedboats roaring across the lake and ice cubes tinkling in the highball glasses of the fly-by-night urban visitors—we knew that summer had arrived. With it came new tasks, problems and surprises for us in both town and forest.

SUMMER

The Hinge

IN OUR LATITUDE, June is the year's hinge and testing time for country dwellers. Now, at the solstice, the planet begins to turn its northern flank slowly away from the sun, and many gardeners turn away from their earthy toil, seeking the toilsome pleasure known as holidays. Though outward signs of change are still faint, the year is running down. Already the annual climax of rustic hope and folly has passed.

Harry Snape was our first neighbour to recognize the planetary shift. Just before sunrise on a glorious June morning I stood on our little balcony sniffing the June attar when Snape strolled down the lane, his military tunic inflated by his illegal shotgun. He stopped to chat with one of the farmer's hired hands who was passing on an empty haywagon, and the two men fell into confidential neighbourhood gossip.

Pointing towards our house, Snape observed: "Why, 'e's mad and she's mad, too. Blowed if they ain't spendin' the summer a-buildin' of a fish pond! So 'elp me, a bloody fish pond, by God!"

This, alas, was true. We were indeed building three adjacent ponds for goldfish by damming hollows in the rocks. When we had built cement walls, hidden them behind second walls of stone and devised a steady drip of water from above, we planted lilies and iris. Finally we installed a score of goldfish and judged the result a triumph of skill. Actually it was a permanent nuisance.

Cats, garter snakes and wandering kingfishers consumed as many goldfish as we bought at the petshops. Tadpoles, imported from the nearest swamp by small boys for ten cents apiece, turned into frogs that promptly disappeared, their homing instinct apparently irresistible. So did a pair of native turtles presented to us by mainland friends. Worst of all, the ponds kept leaking, no matter how often we relined them with waterproof cement. Today they lack fish, frogs and turtles, still leak, but nourish abundant mosquito larvae and confirm Snape's analysis of our youthful madness.

The ponds were not the first among many psychotic symptoms. Even before our house was built I erected a board fence, twelve feet high and forty feet long, with heavy cedar posts and props, to shelter the blossoms of espaliered peach trees from the wind. Most of the blossoms perished in the late spring frosts. We harvested about a dozen peaches in warm years, in cold years none. In due course the peach wall was removed. The labour of reducing it to fuel occupied a complete winter.

Percy Rawling observed these ruins and warned us against additional fantasies.

"N'mind," he said. "Men have always spent their lives in fantasy. What else are wars and politics? What else are business and money? Gar, crazy the whole kit and boilin' of us. Go on then with your next bubble before someone pricks it."

So we did, with repeated follies. It took us several summers to become true country bumpkins. But always we revelled in the opulence of June, that month of scented, almost carnal vegetation when foliage gushes out everywhere like torrents of green liquid.

Nature has produced no perfume sweeter than the breath of new-mown hay. This fact I had known since, as a boy of thirteen years, I learned the use of scythe and pitchfork. With two other boys I helped a poor farmer of the Cowichan Valley to get in his crop because his son was fighting overseas in the First World War. The heat of noonday seemed to bring out the full bouquet of the haycocks as we piled them, sweating and itching, at wages of ten cents an hour, more than the farmer could afford to pay.

In later years, when the hayfields across the land from our Saanich place were cut by a mechanical mower behind a team of Clydesdales, the richly flavoured June air brought back memories unknown to urban folk who had never swung a scythe, filled a loft or sprawled on a haycock watching the night sky fill with stars.

If, said Emerson, the stars appeared only once in a century, all humans would turn out to see them or miss life's supreme experience. But just as the stars are usually taken for granted and ignored, so do urban folk miss the motley June colours and distillations, the mild tincture of blossom, the tang of pine needles, mint and crushed nettles, the manly smell of plowed earth, the homely smell of milk cows grazing on juicy grass and, perhaps best of all to a horseman, the pungent whiff of an old barn, oat bins, leather harness and cattle liniment.

Nothing is more evocative of better days than nature's changing scents. Wild roses at twilight, a salty ocean breeze, campfire smoke or aromatic sage brush may recall in vivid, and often painful, clarity youth's lost hopes and companions.

In the city, the fumes of automobiles, melting asphalt and synthetic female aromas blunt the nose, which no longer detects the clean flavours of the soil. Only a blind man, suddenly acquiring sight, will fully grasp and rejoice in the splendours of the world around him. But even he will not see all the colours or breathe all the scents known to nonhuman creatures. A small fraction of life is visible to any creature, the grand workmanship forever hidden.

Dot and I were too busy in our young days for such speculations. Probably we worked too hard on our garden, and Rawling cautioned us against our excesses.

"You're aging before your time," he said. "You're wearing out." Then, dimpled by his ponderous wit: "Great God, you look like something that came off the horns of a dilemma. Chuck it, my children, chuck it!"

Of course he didn't mean us to chuck it, and of course we never did. In fact he had taught me how to use a shovel with maximum efficiency, as he had mastered it in the mines of Nevada, when the handle is grasped against the knee and a forward thrust of the leg relieves part of the arms' strain.

Even Rawling, who had lifted countless loads of broken rock, had not learned the trick of digging a garden—the wide trench, the quick twist of the shovel to turn the sod upside-down and bury it, the levelling of the surface. But he did understand the value of exercise now that he could no longer enjoy it.

"My boy," he told me, "there's nothing like a good country sweat. It's better than any medicine the doctors know. Sweat and a rum ration! You can't ask more. Ha, what's life for, you ask me"—though I hadn't. "Only three things. Making war, making camp and making love. That covers everything worth your trouble."

Making home and a garden seemed to be an essential aspect of the trinity, and it improved our health. Muscles hardened. Hands blistered and then calloused because no gardener can wear gloves when working with small plants.

But the squalid facts of country life were unknown, I concluded, to the men and women who wrote about them in the skyscrapers of New York. If we had tried to follow a minor fraction of their helpful hints, we would have collapsed among the cabbages or violets. I stopped reading syndicated advice and avoided my father's collection of authentic garden books.

He had become learned in his craft, but there was more to it than technical knowledge and the cunning of his hands. Towards the end he suspected that plants could feel pleasure or hurt. His conscience troubled him, I think, when he ate vegetables.

Long ago he had rejected machinery after buying a second-hand Model T Ford, driving it without incident for a month or two until, pressing his foot on the wrong pedal, he forced himself and the vehicle through the plate-glass windows of a hotel.

He paid for the damage, took the bus home and insisted that I now own the Model T. Accordingly, I drove it to the office every day until its canvas top blew off with a shattering, dynamite blast to terrify pedestrians on crowded Douglas Street. Too humiliated to pause and explain, I drove on. The naked ribs above me seemed to interest all the spectators. Next day I sold the car to an impoverished neighbour for twenty-five dollars and luckily never saw it again.

Before his untimely end, my father's life was lived mostly in the green kingdom, the days with his plants, the evenings with his botanical books. His only irritants were the stray rabbits that nibbled his seedlings, the weevils that destroyed the roots of his primulas, the earwigs that gorged on all blooms and foliage. He could not bear to trap the rabbits and hated to poison the insects, so they multiplied rapidly. Apart from them he had no enemies except, perhaps, a vague and distant political presence in Ottawa, which he called "those Liberal swine."

I had long ceased to kill animals and regretted my boyhood slaughter, with a .22 rifle, of some half dozen fool grouse hens roosting in the trees beside Cowichan Lake. Even now I am occasionally conscience-striken by the memory of my first victim, a blue jay. I killed it for the pleasure of killing. Its glazed, dying eyes as it lay at my feet still horrify me whenever I see a living member of that handsome species in the orchard.

More horrible is the memory of a night in a hayfield with a bush farmer's teen-age son who had an electric torch fastened to his cap. As the rays of this pitlamp moved across the field, they encountered two gleaming spots. Instantly my companion fired his shotgun, the spots disappeared, and we found a deer's carcass not far off. The killer had knowingly broken the law, but only to protect his father's hay crop and secure food for a desperately poor family.

On a later day his dogs treed a cougar. I bravely volunteered to fetch a rifle from the house a mile away. The farm boy was left with the dogs to watch the cougar. When I returned, it was still perched in the crotch of a maple, spitting angrily, baring its teeth and twitching its tail.

The boy sighted his rifle and squeezed the trigger. Blood spurted from the great cat's head and it fell lifeless to the ground. We hung it from a stout pole and carried it home.

Again, there was a good reason for the killing. On every dead cougar the government paid a bounty of forty dollars, a tidy sum to the farmer. Besides, cougars killed his sheep and calves.

By the time I had settled down near Victoria, all thought of killing a creature of any kind, even a mouse or rat in the basement, repelled me. But I remained wildly inconsistent, ate meat and, on camping expeditions, massacred fish wholesale, mostly for sporting fun. There seemed to be—though of course there was not—a moral distinction between cold marine life and warm-blooded animals of the land.

Rawling and I once argued this distinction, and, as always, he had the last word.

"You're a member of the human race, aren't you?" he demanded. "Well, I sometimes wonder. But count on it, humans are carnivores. Therefore they'll kill animals and kill each other, too, in millions, quite legally. We call it war. Yem, yem, there'll be wars so long as men are carnivores. And by God, you're just one of 'em."

Though carnivorous, Dot and I did our best to protect the birds on our land. We fed them grain all winter and in spring rescued fallen baby robins and put them back in their nests. From an upstairs window we observed a pair of hummingbirds create a thimble-sized residence lined with shiny white porcelain. Soon two eggs hatched and released two infants no larger than bumble bees. Next year the same performance unfolded in the same place. Before the third year the nest had been demolished by winter gales.

Until subdivisions began to cut up the farms around us, we never lacked bird song. English skylarks, the only ones then in America, soared high to offer profuse strains of unpremeditated art. But their song, so long continued, became a little monotonous, and we thought it inferior to the bubbling flute music of the native meadowlark.

Both species deserted us when houses and gardens invaded their nesting meadows. The robins, sparrows, juncos, towhees, chickadees, woodpeckers, blue Steller's jays, wrens and ubiquitous crows lingered. But we missed the pheasant's hoarse cry and the treble piping note of the quail.

The bees from a neighbour's commercial hives kept our fruit blossoms well fertilized and never paused in their work to sting us. As we knelt to weed the vegetables we sometimes heard the honeymakers buzzing in the ruddy chalice of a fox-glove flower but, oddly enough, they seemed to prefer above all others the puny cotoneaster blooms that attracted them in murmurous hosts.

Snape's shotgun, it must be recorded in fairness to that military veteran, was not responsible for the demise of our bantam hens.

When some innocent bouquet had been carried from eastern Canada to Vancouver Island and spread a plague of earwigs, the gardeners of Victoria tried every known remedy, including traps and poisons. A last resort and panacea was a flock of dwarf chickens. They would eat the insects and do no harm to vegetation.

Driven to this desperate remedy, we bought a bantam cock named Thunder (for his raucous greeting to the dawn) and a drab, nameless hen. They fed sumptuously on earwigs to produce eggs, hidden in the bush, and then a sizable family.

Within a couple of years our garden, meadow and oak woods swarmed with tiny fowls. The polygamous Thunder protected his increasing harem by fierce crowing sounds, welcomed our handouts of bread crusts and declared his authority at sunrise and frequently during the day.

Vanity was his undoing. Raccoons from Christmas Hill, alerted by his voice, feasted on all our lively pets. One morning we found some scattered red feathers in the rockery. They were all that remained of Thunder.

While Rawling was sympathetic, he noted the carnivorous habits of raccoons. "Yem, yem, just like us," he said.

His remark was somewhat callous, but we now had to grapple at our camp with a process much larger and longer than the lives of bantams or humans.

At the
Peak

IN EARLY SUMMER the forest's growth is at its annual peak. So is man's genius for destruction as he expunges nature's work of centuries.

From around our camp the first loggers had departed long ago, leaving behind them some fifty trees too big for their axes, handsaws, oxen and skid roads. Now we lived mostly among second-growth, already fit for a lumber mill if we would sell it.

Of course we didn't, but a mile along the road a wealthy resident beside the lake offered, quite unawares, the synopsis and metaphor of coastal history.

To provide space for a two-car garage, it was necessary to remove a cedar about six feet in diameter at shoulder height. Accordingly, an expert logger was summoned. His chainsaw made the undercut in ten minutes. The falling cut, on the opposite side, took nearly an hour. A steel wedge was inserted, a maul drove it in about two inches. The cedar swayed, its torn wood screamed, its wings beat as if for flight. When it fell across the road the earth boomed like a drum. That expert had done his work well. There was plenty of room for the garage.

On the stump we counted the wide growth rings of summer, the narrow rings of winter. Wet and dry years were fixed by this climatic record. The tree was more than seven centuries old, though we could not tell exactly because some rings at the outer edge were too fine for the naked eye.

King John must have been signing a certain document at Runnymede when a seed sprouted in a forest unknown to any white man. When Columbus discovered a new continent, the cedar was growing fast. But growth had slowed down by the time of Waterloo, and in our time had almost ceased.

Through all those centuries—a momentary span in geological history but long in human experience—the tree had been the harp of spring winds, the pipe organ of winter gales. It had sucked from the earth water and chemicals beyond reckoning. With this nourishment it had formed heartwood, a moist cambium layer, a network of reddish bark and plumes of green needles. It had absorbed carbon, discharged oxygen into the air and helped to sustain animal life on a then-unpolluted planet.

Thus cell by cell it kept expanding its bulk when no man had yet seen it. The Indians always avoided a region where evil spirits lurked, and white men did not reach here before the middle of the nineteenth century. So the tree was left alone to bear the crushing load of winter snow and survive killing summer drought. Anchored and nourished by a fine filament of roots, it defied the law of gravity.

When competitors languished and died in its shade, the cedar ate their mouldering bodies and converted them into living substance. It unknowingly depicted a process that began with the retreat of the glaciers some ten thousand years ago.

Slowly the southern forest crept northward long before humans had built their first town and devised their first alphabet. When the march of immigrants reached here, only yesterday, across the Bering landbridge, most of them shunned this eerie jungle, living instead on the seashore or travelling southward to warmer climates. Even today's inhabitants can find the forest daunting.

In winter, a city man entering the woods is likely to suffer claustrophobia and hastens away from an unseen ghostly presence. In summer, the forest seems to relax its brooding malevolence and the trespasser's claustrophobia relaxes, too. At no season do the forest's labour and growth ever pause. When its needles and leaves drop and it looks idle, its roots are spreading underground. Fat, sleek-headed mankind sleeps o' nights, the forest never.

Its unwanted human companions around the lake varied in character and occupation.

The most notable of all residents was Gordon Hunter, the chief justice of the British Columbia Supreme Court, whose summer place included half a dozen cottages and a huge workshop full of machinery for the production of artistic wooden and metallic objects. From it emerged, so far as his widow could remember, only a pair of copper lamp shades worth a dollar each, at most.

Hunter installed an ancient cannon on his lawn as if to repel invaders from the lake. Nearby, a lion made of concrete and twice life-size also guarded the premises. A well was drilled through solid rock and a windmill erected to supply pure water for the judge's tea or, mixed with whiskey, for his evening comfort.

Despite these eccentricities, Hunter was a natural country man. In ragged overalls he worked beside his two Japanese servants, Frankie and Namura, to improve the gardens or clear more land. If visitors appeared, he often posed as a hired hand who spoke little English. The chief justice, he said, was in Nanaimo or Kamloops.

That another judge of the same rank would follow Hunter into his favourite region could not have occurred to him or, in our early years, to us. But in due time John Owen Wilson, a friend from my childhood and one of Hunter's successors on the bench, visited our place at every chance, swam in the lake, paddled the canoe and, working alone, grubbed out a trail of half a mile to encircle the property. With an eight-foot double-ended saw he and I felled and cut up many dead trees, split them with wedge and maul, lugged them, chunk by chunk, out of the tangled brush and exhausted ourselves.

Wilson's intimate, John Valentine Clyne, had left the bench to become the chief executive of a great forest empire, and occasionally he would fly from Vancouver and swoop down on the lake in his plane for a quiet holiday. The operator of logging camps, sawmills, paper mills and assorted industries in several countries joined us at the saw and chopping block. But on one stifling hot summer day, after his plane was moored to our wharf, he stepped ashore swathed in a thick woollen scarf, and we saw that he could barely turn his head.

"Stiff neck," was all he said, for Clyne never complained of his health even in times of grave illness. On this occasion both he and Wilson were lucky to find in our cabin the wife of a famous Cariboo rancher, a woman of long experience with pain, accidents and frontier remedies.

Halcyon Carson took charge immediately. She ordered the chief justice, whose back was cramped by toil in the woods, and the stiff-necked timber baron to remove their shirts, forced them to lie face-down on the couches and demanded a supply of the hottest water available. Dot provided it from the kitchen kettle. Halcyon wetted towels and applied one of them to Clyne's neck, the other to Wilson's spine, ignoring the screams of agony that shot from the two scalded Jacks. Then she twisted Clyne's head until it seemed likely to fall off and pommelled Wilson's back with her fists.

Any newspaper in Canada would have paid a high price for a photograph of these eminent, half-naked and writhing British Columbians, but, disloyal to my own publisher, I did not report the incident. And after a little while, both of Halcyon's patients fully recovered.

My most frequent helper and faithful friend was a professor of economics at the Royal Military College outside Victoria. While Dr. Alfred Carlsen practised his dismal science, his real interest, like mine, was the outdoors, and he had worked in it since boyhood on his Norwegian parents' stump ranch north of Vancouver. No other man of my acquaintance was so expert with axe and saw. None enjoyed this work so much. His departure left a gap in our woodpiles and, more importantly, in our lives.

Over the years some unlikely persons drifted by.

J. B. Priestley, the English author, paused at the camp long enough to explain that time stands still, its passage an illusion of the human mind. In proof of his theory he rearranged the dinner plates, knives and forks in a circular pattern and was surprised when we could not understand him.

One of our most notable visitors was Yousuf Karsh, the photographer of worldwide renown, who arrived with two assistants, a policeman from Victoria as body guard and our wheelbarrow full of cameras, reflecting mirrors and electrical gadgets. The native Armenian boy who made himself a great Canadian artist was taking scenic pictures for *Maclean's* magazine, and he went promptly to work.

Seeing at once that the five handsome arbutus trees at the edge of the patio formed a natural frame for the lake, Yousuf focussed his lights and camera on them while we observed him in silence. But something was wrong. The trunks of the arbutus, he said, were not glossy enough. Looking around, he noticed a man in torn and grimy clothing who stood behind the others, obviously a hired roustabout.

"Get a hose," Yousuf ordered. "Wet the trees down. And hurry."

The roustabout obediently sprayed the arbutus trunks until they glistened in the sun. Yousuf hid his head under a black cloth and took a dozen camera shots of trees and lake. He was soon lost in the frenzy of his art and bathed in sweat. When he had finished at last I took him by the arm and led him to the silent roustabout.

"Yousuf," I said, "allow me to present Chief Justice Wilson of the Supreme Court."

Yousuf stared at Wilson for a brief moment.

"Oh God!" he muttered and without another word ran down to the wharf and, fully clothed, jumped into the lake.

"Ah well," said Wilson, the inveterate punster, "I'll take the Karsh and let the credit go."

Of all the lakeshore residents, Ray Dougan, a man of burly figure and red cheeks, was the most successful and beloved. In his big garage he and his apprentices repaired logging trucks, tractors, automobiles, radios and television sets. Ray could fix anything. With the necessary education he might have been a nuclear physicist but, lacking it, he put his five children through university and saw them in learned professions. He built the village waterworks, organized the volunteer fire department and made a tank truck with pumping equipment. Though he also built a luxurious camper, he preferred to take his holidays travelling across the country on a motorcycle, his goodly wife perched behind him.

Ray never failed us. When our electric pump stopped working on a memorable Sunday and our cabin was crammed with guests, he left his midday meal, drove to our place and discovered that a tiny but vital part of the machine was broken. A replacement, he said, must be flown from Toronto with the delay of maybe a week. But on second thoughts, he carried the whole pump to my crude workshop, where, using a piece of copper and a file, he manufactured the needed part and installed it. The pump has worked satisfactorily ever since.

Because I was no good with machinery, I distrusted it, even after our habits had become shamefully decadent and the cabin rebuilt, enlarged, electrified, filled with sunlight and equipped with a telephone. No longer had I to use Dougan's garage three miles away for the unavoidable long-distance calls of my trade. He no longer had to send a messenger (for a charge of one dollar) to tell me that the office in Victoria or Winnipeg was calling.

If I could not operate a machine more complex than a wheelbarrow or a grindstone, I was turning into a fairly competent woodworker and mason. Doubtless my over-weening pride in these crafts was repulsive, but I was more competent at them than at my typewriter.

Obsessed with the need of privacy, Dot and I acquired for a song (by cable from Paris, oddly enough) the cabin next to ours. Returning home, we found that the purchase seemed likely to tumble down without warning.

I had to crawl beneath the crazy structure to replace the log foundation posts. They were rotten because the builder had not taken the trouble to skin them. My crawling job took all one summer. Next year Wilson and I propped up the roof of the verandah, God knows how, removed the corner posts, also unskinned, and inserted heavy, skinned timbers from the forest.

By now the stone fireplace was disintegrating, the mortar falling out. Though I had never used cement nor heard the word *grout,* I bought a trowel and spent a full month filling the cracks until the fireplace and its tall chimney were safe.

My labours had only begun. Too late, I realized that I should have razed the cabin and started building afresh. It took me three summers to gut its insides, reline them with yellow cedar, add a kitchen and a bathroom, fashion bunks, cupboards and bookcases and hew a mantel shelf out of a fir log.

Even then the absurd project was not finished. For the use of my newly married son and his wife, I undertook to build a large sundeck if he would manhandle the necessary beams and floor planks over a rough trail a quarter of a mile long. Roping them to our wheelbarrow, he somehow brought them in. By the summer's end, the deck, resting on solid concrete foundations, seemed to justify our efforts, and it was to serve two more generations of the tribe.

Much other work had been done already—three wharfs, a woodshed, a workshop, a boathouse high above the lake with a runway of squared logs and a cradle on wheels for launching the boats, a dressing hut for swimmers and more than a hundred pieces of furniture, not elegant but strong and durable.

One of the earliest and the hardest jobs of all was a guest hut. I dragged its log uprights, beams and rafters from the woods and lifted them by ropes and pulleys because, in those days, I had no one to help me. For the walls I bought an abandoned garage, at a cost of four dollars, and carried its sound boards half a mile from the main road.

Long before our original cabin had been rebuilt, we devised a primitive apparatus to cool perishable foodstuffs. The oil drum on stilts, filled with water that we pumped by hand from the lake, supplied a flat metal tank over a porch cupboard swathed in burlap. As the cloth sucked moisture from the tank, it was slightly chilled by evaporation. Our rudimentary refrigerator wasn't much good, but it kept meat from spoiling and butter from liquefying for a couple of days if we constantly replenished the oil drum.

When our kids and their friends were old enough to be conscripted for child labour, I undertook perhaps my craziest job. From a dead but sound fir tree I shaped four flat pieces, each ten feet long, two feet wide and a foot thick. We laid down pieces of small skinned and slippery trees to make a kind of skid road. A dozen boys and girls, and several adults, heaving on a rope, dragged the hewn timbers to the cabin. As steps to the verandah they looked mighty fine, but split and rotted in about ten years. This time, I had enough sense to replace them with squared and planed beams specially cut by a local sawmill. My use of broad-axe and child labour was not repeated.

Of necessity I worked with stone, too. Retaining walls were easy to build once I learned to mix cement and sand in the right proportions. But to find enough smooth rocks for a patio about thirty feet square, bring them out of the woods in the wheel-barrow and lay them with a surface approximately level was a task for two summers.

On bruised knees, my hands raw from sharp boulders, I wist-fully imagined that, long after most human remains had dis-appeared, some alien archaeologists might penetrate a new jungle, stumble on my stonework and puzzle over it. Here, one of them would say, barbarian creatures probably sacrificed young virgins to bloodthirsty gods, or glaciers and earthquakes had accidentally deposited the stones in a rough pattern. No, no, a second investigator argues, sentient beings, not quite hu-man but superior to most animals, lived here before civilized men poisoned the planet and almost destroyed their species.

If such a future argument was improbable, my walls and patio (unlike newspaper columns that perished in a single day) would last for several generations. It is surprising what a man can do over six decades; surprising also that he takes more enjoyment in a spare-time hobby than in his trade. Most surprising of all is the collapse of his energies after middle age and, with them, his vainglory.

Still, the outdoor man who uses his hands more than his brain feels a certain pity for the handless indoor intellectuals. But men and women who govern the nation or manage its industry seem to enjoy themselves. I did not envy their exercise of power and admired their sacrifice of higher enjoyment.

After some four decades in our camp, I lacked an office for my neglected livelihood of journalism. Dot and I chose a site for this final job at the lakeshore, cleared away brush and dislodged inconvenient stones with a crowbar. In two summers of work alone I built the office, panelled it with red cedar boards and attached a sleeping porch some ten feet above the water.

Now, in the darkness, we could hear wavelets gurgling against the rocks, the stealthy creep of raccoons searching for crayfish, the click of their teeth as they ate their prey, the splash of a mink under the wharf and then, from the flank of the mountain, the stutter of the midnight freight train.

It was climbing the steepest commercial grade in Canada towards Cliffside Station where, in August 1886, Sir John A. Macdonald had driven the last spike of the Esquimalt and Nanaimo Railway.

Following such rare physical exertion, he badly needed a drink. There was none on the special train, but Robert Dunsmuir, owner of the railway, and also thirsting, had planned a joint rescue mission. When the train reached Nanaimo, he led his guest deep down into his coal mine, safe from their teetotalling wives, and provided lavish refreshments, liquid and solid. Both men, it is said, returned to the surface in a genial mood.

Only in our time was the historic site of Cliffside marked by a stone cairn and a bronze tablet. By then the station, a wooden shed, was flat on the ground. The daily passenger train seldom stopped there, and the steam locomotive struggled desperately to reach the summit, wheels spinning on the tracks. As it touched the crest its whistle blared out its immemorial greeting.

For old Canadians, the steam locomotive, unique among machines, was almost a living thing, a friend and faithful servant. Its whistle, echoing and re-echoing in the mountains, assured the pioneers that the scattered habitations of their lonely land were grappled together with hoops of steel. As much as governments, railways created and preserved the nation.

Today no steam locomotives pass deserted Cliffside. Their successors, the diesels, easily climb the summit and blow their steamless whistles in poor imitation of that authentic and triumphant note unknown to the young generation.

As a change from my role as amateur mason and carpenter, I sometimes fooled with small, and preferably old, leaky boats.

This work is simple and good for the soul. While he mends, caulks, patches and paints a boat, the owner finds parables and secret meanings. If a mouldering punt has been kept afloat long enough, year after year, it becomes not only a friend but a true allegory of the human condition, that perpetual tragicomedy in all its despair and glory.

The man fixing the punt knows that he, too, requires patches on the chinks of his splintered life. He knows, better than the dwellers in the make-believe security of streets, that every living thing wears out. Mankind's neglect must be repaired, if possible, its blunders briefly disguised with paint.

An old man is largely made up of patches, and soon the day will come when, like his boat, he will be left forgotten on the shore. Thus the patcher, painter and caulker, given sufficient annual experience, graduates as a philospher and vicarious adventurer.

Man and boat are going nowhere, but he dreams of far-off seas, the green islands of the south, the Vikings and pirates, his ancestors of the north. In their youth all men make brave plans for life's voyage, with cargoes of virtuous intention, rich assorted goods for trade with the natives. Alas, few men and boats escape from their wharfs and moorings.

To me, boats and cabins were among the few stable things left in a mad, reeling world to indicate the quiet, abiding rhythm that endures beneath the outward disorder of our times. Other men find this comfort in churches, money, power or drink. Let them find it where they can. I found it now and then, not always, when I had shucked off the garments of society, the masks and flatulent pretensions.

Reality seemed to await me at the trail's end, the water's edge. And I wished that our statesmen would sometimes absent themselves from Ottawa's felicity awhile to paint a worthless boat. Thus they might rediscover their youthful dreams, and a whiff of authentic Canada would enter the governing system.

These, of course, were my private fantasies, disclosed to nobody. But as the parent of a seven-year-old son, I had to consider his maritime ambitions. Already possessing a flat-bottomed craft, he rigged up a mast, attached a piece of canvas and decorated the hull in blue and red stripes. With a big circle of yellow on either side, he revealed to us his masterpiece, the *Golden Dawn*.

It didn't satisfy him for long. When he observed a sailboat, about ten feet in length, riding at anchor for weeks across the lake, he knew that it rightfully belonged to him. Sure enough, the owner was glad to sell it for fifty dollars, though its sail alone was worth much more than that.

After the deal was completed with five minutes' talk, the boy lived most of the summer on his trim vessel and seldom capsized it more than once a day. He was accompanied by his water spaniel, appropriately called Skipper. If the wind dropped, the dog would plunge into the lake and swim ashore, while the navigator would also swim, towing the boat home by a rope gripped in his teeth. Or if he tired of this exertion, his sister, now ten years old and virtually amphibious, would relieve him and return from a mile's cruise in the same fashion.

Naturally, I inherited the *Golden Dawn,* half sunk, and salvaged her for no good reason. Those were the days before the internal combustion engine was perfected. A dozen launches with quiet inboard motors and some rowboats with outboards about as powerful as eggbeaters were the only craft propelled by gasoline.

Progress launched the first speedboats of hideous sound and nauseating vapour, and they drove away the loons, with their haunting laugh, and the trout deep down in the lake. By now most of the canoes had disappeared, too, intimidated by the threat of youngsters riding water skis in wild tangents and jets of foam. Sometimes, in the dusk, when the lake was deserted and calm again, some daring canoes would venture from their daylight refuge. Apparently breeding in secret, they continued to increase, but their new structure of metal or fibreglass could not satisfy a veteran paddler who had loved the original cedar-strip variety, an art form almost as native to Canada as birch-bark.

An old-timer noticed that the young canoeists, while their revulsion against machinery was encouraging, had yet to learn the skill of the paddle. They bent and unnecessarily tired their arms and often steered by shifting their paddles from one side of the canoe to the other. The pity of it.

So far has the young generation departed from the old, but even the survival of the canoe in any form is another parable, like the leaky boat. For those who know Canadian history, the canoe symbolizes the endurance of the nation and the quality of the folk who made it.

The days of early summer and rampant vegetable life kept reminding us of time's swift passage.

Sword ferns were as high as a man's chest. Pale trilliums had turned purple and then dropped their blooms. Yellow violets and pink bleeding hearts had gone from the swamp margin. Broom shrubs beside every road had lost the gold of spring and hurled their seeds, by noiseless explosion, a distance of several feet to spread their progeny. Now came blue lupin, maroon fireweed, black-spotted orange tiger lilies and miles of white daisies.

Equally white, Indian pipes thrust up their waxen, fungus-like blossoms in damp, shady places. Scarlet Indian paintbrush hugged the beach at high-water mark. Along the forest trails we found tiny, nameless growths of many colours; they would have been weeds in town. Here they displayed their true beauty to our sated, purblind eyes.

By late July the season of drought was upon us. The woods thirsted for rain under a hard, cloudless sky. The smallest spark from a chimney or a discarded cigarette butt could set the trees aflame. Reluctantly we left nature's garden for a few days at a time to cultivate and water our poor man-made imitation outside Victoria. But we soon returned, happy in our escape from society.

The
Halcyon
Days

IF WE WERE LIVING in the forest, our place near town was protected against burglars and vandals by a friend, a neighbour and
one of nature's noblemen.

George Rogers inherited his father's farm of several hundred
acres. In the days of Fort Victoria, they had been a segment of
the Hudson's Bay Company's estate and now stretched from
Christmas Hill across a rough gravel road that was to become a
major highway. The original Rogers farmhouse stood beside
the tracks of the Victoria and Sidney Railway. Its train, pulled
by a wood-burning locomotive, stopped to pick up young
George and his siblings when they planned a visit to town.

After his parents' death, George, newly married, built a house
for himself and his wife opposite us on the lane soon to be offi-
cially gazetted as Rogers Avenue. From then on he not only
watched our property but rescued us from accidents like broken
water pipes, clogged drains or cranky automobile engines. He
was a jack-of-all-trades, but would accept no payment for his
trouble.

To me this tall, gaunt and silent man, following his sleek
Clydesdales and plow, sowing grain by hand, cutting hay, reaping autumn crops or filling his silo with chopped corn, was the
living portrait of the Canadian farm breed, the unconscious heir

to Louis Hébert, who first broke the sod of Champlain's colony at Quebec.

George had no time for such historical reflections. With his three hired men, he was busy feeding and milking some thirty cows, bottling the milk, and delivering it in his truck all over Victoria when his customers were still abed. After breakfast and a nap, the day's routine began. Even after he had replaced his Clydesdales with a powerful tractor and installed milking machines, the farm work was too heavy for any man's strength. But George never missed Sunday service in the Saanich pioneers' little church.

His farm prospered. His Jersey herd multiplied. His tawny cows and calves grazing on a green field cheered us at many a summer sunrise. His children played with ours in the hayloft, the orchard and the oak groves of Christmas Hill. A supposedly savage Jersey bull let them ride on his back without complaint.

For country kids this was indeed a halcyon time. They lived on a vitamin-rich diet before vitamins had appeared in common speech and, unlike kids nowadays, they drank undiluted milk, its cream filling a third of the quart bottle.

Busy as he was, George never failed at night to record the day's weather and the state of the crops. His diary over a period of two score years showed that the local climate was changing.

In the time of Fort Victoria, winters were cold, every farmer had a sleigh, the Fraser River sometimes froze at its mouth, ships were forced to dock in Burrard Inlet and the Douglas Road was built from there to New Westminster. Around mid-century a different cycle began, average temperature rose and the growing season lengthened. In our time, as George recorded it, the climate entered another down cycle, and the average growing season lost some hours each year.

Urban folk did not observe the change, but its effects on his crops were important to George and even to me in my vegetable patch where I found that squash, marrows, cucumbers and tomatoes often lacked enough sunshine and warmth.

A garden brings out the best and the worst qualities of the gardener. I was lavish with my gifts of vegetables, but expected visitors to commend my flowers. When they didn't pause to notice them, my secret vanity was offended until I learned that the true rewards of gardening, as of any work, were solitary. If a man cannot enjoy his garden alone, without specious flattery, he had better not plant it. All this I was to understand only in a future solitude unforeseeable in my salad days.

Even the gardener innocent of vanity and misanthropic by nature is sure to overestimate his strength of body and mind. At the beginning, Dot and I planted an area far too big for proper maintenance, no matter how hard we toiled. Our tastes were also extravagant, running to gaudy perennials and blocks of mixed primary colours that fastidious gardeners might regret as vulgar. In our unsophisticated eyes the hues of vegetation could not clash. We liked them all, singly or together.

As the years passed and our energies declined, we had the sense at last to eliminate the smaller, fussier plants and let vigorous shrubs take their place. Our vegetable patch gradually shrank. But the dawn of outdoor reality, and perhaps sanity, was still a long way ahead in the happiest years of our joint life.

At this stage we indulged numerous follies, like putting potatoes and carrots under hay and mounds of earth as we had seen Rogers doing to preserve his crops for later sale. My energies were then so robust that I climbed a hundred-foot fir tree just to get a spacious view of the countryside—an absurd exercise—long before the tree was killed, with others, by devouring insects.

To Percy Rawling our whole undertaking was absurd. Why labour for vegetables, he demanded, when they could be bought cheaply in the shops and were doubtless of superior quality? Poison gas having destroyed his sense of smell, his palate was dulled, and I don't think he believed our contention that corn, spinach, peas or beans, cooked within five minutes of their picking, had a flavour lost after a few hours in storage. But he was reconciled to our habits and enjoyed our vegetables even if they seemed no better than his usual restaurant fare.

All our planting, cultivating, weeding and harvesting represented a pathetic miniature of Canada's food industry. Most people observe from trains, buses or airplanes the Okanagan orchards heavy with fruit, the Cariboo ranges and Alberta foothills with their fattening cattle, the prairies in spring greenery or autumn gold, the lush dairy farms of Ontario and Quebec, the broad potato fields and narrow seaside plots of the Maritimes.

After Dot and I travelled by automobile from coast to coast and detoured north and south for thousands of miles, we had at least some notion of the labour and the gamble against weather or fluctuating prices needed to produce Canada's food.

So vast is the country, so widely separated its nodules of population, so varied its origins, attitudes and lifeways, that with all its machinery of communication the different regions sometimes feel like strangers to one another.

The minute corner legally, but so temporarily, possessed by Dot and me had its ups and downs, happiness and heartbreak.

"You young buggers 'ave all the luck," Harry Snape told me when his military pension was eroded by the fall of Britain's currency. "But wait. You'll get yours one of these days."

That warning seemed to offer him much satisfaction. Naturally, we disregarded it. Almost half a century of life together gave us more contentment and supposed security than we deserved.

But in the years of economic turmoil, war and revolution, our once quiet and empty neighbourhood could not avoid the course of human events.

Until the great North American boom turned into a great bust, Victoria grew fast, engorging the countryside, covering the farmland with paved streets, houses and stores. Our rusticity began to wear thin, but our privacy was shielded by Rogers's acreage and the oak groves.

A charming little Frenchman named Jules Fairee (as we vaguely understood his accent) built a bungalow at the edge of our property. He was a barber and hair stylist by profession, and by Gallic heritage a logician who designed his garden according to the laws of Euclid. His bulbs, perennials and shrubs were laid out in straight lines, the Euclidean shortest distance between two points. The result was a neat geometrical equation, and though he was too polite to mention our disorderly methods, we knew they outraged his sense of order and decorum.

Near him, an expert horticulturist and strict teetotaller from England, whose name I forget, planted several acres of loganberry bushes to supply the new wine factory at Lake Hill. After the repeal of Prohibition, loganberry wine was popular and cheap, though not sufficiently alcoholic to suit the Vancouver Island logging camps. But spiked with rum or whiskey, it produced an explosive beverage called goof. A few pulls of goof would floor the strongest logger.

The loganberry cult didn't last long and was replaced by more sophisticated wines from Europe. Many of the Island bushes were attacked by an incurable virus known as dry berry that shrivelled all my logans and then my raspberries. Since Rogers's bushes were immune to the disease but, transplanted to our garden, quickly withered, I realized that in nature and country life justice is peculiarly blind.

The next house in our district, a botched job of discordant gables, suffered frequent changes of ownership and a mysterious hex.

When the only son of the original owners drowned in a boating accident, the parents sold out and moved away. A fidgety, retired banker from Colorado bought the place and built a greenhouse to serve his hobby of orchid culture until the heating system failed and his treasures froze. With his angular, strong-minded wife, he then returned to Colorado.

A procession of owners continued, and Jerome Pigott arrived to the general regret of the neighbours. A cadaverous creature of shiny, cannonball head ringed by yellow curls, he quickly informed us of his notable teaching career in Nova Scotia. Having acquired a plenteous store of irrelevant knowledge, he generously shared it with anyone willing to listen.

Every day or two, Pigott marched up the lane, observed Dot and me at work in the garden and offered some choice bit of information as if it had just come accidently to his mind.

Thus we learned that Lincoln's famous Emancipation Proclamation affected only slaves in the rebellious southern states where he had no means of enforcing it, that, contrary to legend, Napoleon was not afflicted by hemorrhoids at Waterloo, that Wellington was the tallest man in his army at five feet nine inches, that the Mongol empire of Genghis Khan lasted no more than two centuries, that the people of Quebec must be compelled to speak English, that Canada should abolish its monarchy and create a truly democratic republic.

After listening to Pigott one day without comment, Rawling dredged up the pertinent quotation: "And still they gazed, and still the wonder grew, that one small head could carry all he knew. Gar, this fellow's worse than a pedant. He's a fraud. He has a cheap encyclopaedia and reads up some silly item and spreads it about to split the ears of the groundlings. Why, if any idea got into his skull it'd burst. Ignore him."

It was impossible to ignore Pigott since he always approached us with stealth before we could escape. But finally he, too, moved away.

His house was then bought, or at least occupied, by an ugly, middle-aged woman and three good-looking young ones. They erected a little stone pyramid topped by an electric lantern beside their gate, and at night the driveway was soon full of automobiles. The pyramid attracted numerous clients before the police interrupted the business and the women departed.

After our only brush with commercial vice, an old couple from Saskatchewan bought the house and exorcised its ghosts. The newcomers were accustomed to a full section of wheatland, hard work and the fierce prairie climate. The easy life, soft weather and the claustrophobic oak woods oppressed them until they began to rescue their two acres from years of neglect.

At the public library they borrowed garden books, sought advice even from us, planted fruit trees, shrubs, roses and flowers of all kinds and, inevitably, more vegetables than they could eat. When he could find no job to do on his place, the husband would pull up mustard weeds along the road to prevent them from spreading. If his wife faced an idle hour, she baked cookies for the neighbourhood kids, who adored her.

By this time our daughter, Joan, was about seven years old and our son, Robert, four. They took naturally to rustic life, and their adventures, suitably embellished, gave me endless columns in the newspaper.

None of them is worth repeating, but I cannot forget the tragedy of a little white mongrel pup that Joan described as the offspring of "a rough-haired terror when his father wasn't there." The pup slipped through the ice of the winter swamp and drowned. Trying to save him, all the kids were soaked and went home crying and shivering.

My account of this episode seemed to move the whole neighbourhood and even the callous city. For once I hit a high note.

The mongrel was buried in an apple box under a cross made of two broken laths. To record the melancholy occasion I wrote a real tearjerker. After second thoughts, I realized that it verged on the maudlin. But my beloved mother read it in tears and pasted the ghastly column in her scrapbook of memorabilia.

Rawling took a darker view. Now writing editorials in Vancouver for the *Province,* he often visited us and denounced me for what he called cannibalism in print.

"You know what you're doing?" he protested. "You're livin' off your own children like an animal eatin' its young. If they ever read this slimy stuff they'll never forgive you. Gar, you've left a blot on the English language. And by God, when you grow up it'll haunt you."

Oddly enough, it didn't. At least, not much. And, as Dot observed, "Percy says lots of things he disagrees with."

Benny Nicholas said nothing about my copy in his paper, but he printed it without alteration, made friends of our children, brought them forbidden candy and no longer seemed to fear the poisons of the country air.

He would arrive at our place (or the lieutenant governor's mansion) in a dilapidated Model T Ford, because an old friend and war veteran drove it as a taxi. Hot-tempered, soft-hearted and lonely under his boisterous public guise, Benny had bought a cottage for a poor immigrant widow and her numerous brood. He often visited them to play cards, tell stories or sing opera arias in his rich tenor.

As all parents find, children become adults too quickly. It was amazing to see Robert in university and the Olympic Games, and Joan earning her nurse's degree. Dot and I were also changing and losing some of our vigour.

To replace it I bought a cultivating machine and followed it on foot, grasping the handles, guiding the sharp harrow points and sometimes damaging the fruit trees. From this midget tractor I learned an implacable hatred of mechanical devices.

One hot summer day the tractor's engine stopped running. I pulled the starting cord until I could pull no more, but nothing happened. Robert came to my rescue, disassembled the entire apparatus, laid the parts on the driveway, put them together again and assured me that the machine was as good as new.

He pulled the cord—and still nothing happened. He tightened nuts, adjusted gears and oiled bearings, all in vain. Even when a minor part that had been left on the driveway was installed, the engine wouldn't start. Whereupon, as an expert rugby player, he aimed a mighty kick at the tractor. It sprang to life and afterwards behaved perfectly. Now, for the first time, I appreciated the value of a university education. Students are trained in the vital necessities of life.

In their decisive years, Dot and I made sure that our children knew more about the wilderness than they saw at our camp. We took them on real camping trips, with riding and pack horses and some memorable guides, to the mountains and upland fishing lakes of the Cariboo. There we slept under canvas on beds of sweet-smelling evergreen boughs, caught trout and cooked them on willow twigs over a wood fire.

In Canada, a nation so young, so close to the pioneers who made it, millions of kids have known nothing better than crowded government campgrounds with running water, free firewood and the cacophony of radio music.

This isn't good enough for the pioneers' descendants. A just society (if such a thing is imaginable) would invest in true camps and expose all youngsters to the wilderness in the summer. Thus the nation would earn future dividends and improve its character generation by generation. But our society, so rich in temporary goods, so neglectful of its permanent assets, lacks the wisdom for an obvious and profitable reform.

After our own expeditions far past any road, we returned to the Island forests and in the parched summers watched the giants fight for survival.

The Big Thirst

IN AUGUST CAME the drought. We could almost hear the forest panting, choking and smothering as its thirsty root web sucked up from parched soil the last drops of summer rain. Even the forest's scent had changed. It was no longer soothing to the nostrils but sharp, biting, acrid.

The fight for survival had reached a decisive stage for trees, animals and insects alike. Evergreens shed their needles and from their wounds oozed gobs of sticky resin. In the swamp the proud ferns were disarmed, swords flat on the ground. Nettles withered and lost their sting. Tough leaves of salal drooped, limp and juiceless. Dead branches rubbed together, crackling in the wind. At night, deer coming to drink from the lake seemed to trample the path like horses. The restless feet of squirrels and shrews rustled noisily on dry twigs. Only the ants and invisible bacteria were silent now.

Still the forest pumped up tons of liquid every day. But the battle raging around our cabin was deadly. It involved, on a single acre, more fighters than all the human inhabitants of the world.

Throughout different climates, countries and continents, the same struggle, aggravated by man's ravenous greed, must destroy or preserve the delicately balanced ecosystem that nourishes living creatures of all species. Here, in late summer drought, we saw a microcosm of the planet's dubious fate.

Since winter we had watched an inch or two of pale green on the branch-tips of old conifers. Young ones raised leading shoots three or four feet high. The growth rate varied widely. Wilson and I once cut up a fallen fir two feet in diameter, and it had lived about thirty years. Its growth was too fast in rich soil, its roots too weak for the struggle. But a jack pine, taking root on some twelve square feet of naked stone in the middle of the lake, had reached only a man's height in six decades. It made its own soil by the drop of its needles, and fed a little patch of grass and vagrant blackberry vines. That pine, a landmark to boatmen, was like an outsized bonsai. Skilled Japanese hands might have pruned its roots and dwarfed it. In fact, nature had planted, shaped and then barely tolerated such a brash intruder.

Elsewhere the forest was rank and ruthless as it methodically starved its weak members to death. Only the strong could survive the unequal distribution of soil, sunlight and moisture, but this Darwinian process was slow and unobserved by casual visitors.

They saw the outward stage spectacle, not the cunning arrangements and secret equipment behind the curtain. As the year advanced, the upright cones of the evergreens turned down, each protected against the winter by its tight shingles. Already, seeds of the forest family rode the wind or were carried in bird droppings to germinate miles distant. When trees fell, the bacteria went to work reducing them to nutriment for vegetable life. Ants bored tunnels and built their cities in some rotting log. On its surface or an old stump, infant firs, cedars and hemlocks sprouted and pushed their roots down into the earth. Everywhere leaves grasped the sunlight and, by photosynthesis, mixed water and carbon to form essential carbohydrates.

There is a darker side to this process. Not only man but insects, spores, viruses and microorganisms of numerous varieties attack even the strongest trees. Blister rust has killed most of the highly valued white pines of Vancouver Island and doomed the rest. Butt rot, special enemy of the firs, often topples a giant that appears to be in vigorous health.

If cleanly cut down, a fir sometimes can join its roots to those of a neighbour in symbiotic union and cover its stump with a layer of bark. Healthy conifers usually heal the wounds of storm or man's trespass. If wind tears off a branch, leaving a gash on the trunk, it closes like human lips. But when a deciduous—maple, alder or willow—is felled, the sap within it keeps the leaves green for a little while. The tree, ignorant of its fate, offers a paradigm of human life. Then the amateur woodsman remembers his own chances and hazards.

He, too, is sometimes at peril in the woods. One day when I was young and careless, I swung my axe at an upright dead alder, thinking it would make good fuel. In a fraction of a second the top of the tree, about six feet of it, weighing hundreds of pounds, fell straight down to skin my nose and miss my skull by less than an inch. After that, I kept a safe distance from dead alders and left them to fall without my help.

Among the forest's dwellers the arbutus is the most remarkable. It grows on the coastal shelf north from California to the middle of Vancouver Island, needs dry, gritty soil and, in its first years, drives down a tap root many times the length of its trunk. When it has slowly grown into a sizable tree, its bark is of a colour defined by no dictionary and worn by no other species. Reddish cinnamon is perhaps the closest approximation. Then, as the tissue-thin outer bark peels off in ribbons, it exposes a soft green also without name. Soon it takes on the tree's permanent hue.

No artist, not even Emily Carr with her mystical understanding of the forest, has yet been able to paint the play of sun and shadow on the silken, female contours of the arbutus, and no camera does it justice. But the arbutus has an inconvenient habit of dropping last year's foliage on roofs and patios at midsummer and replacing it with crisp new leaves. In spite of its deciduous look, the tree is an evergreen. Its wood, though easily smoothed by a plane, always cracks and is useless in furniture. Otherwise the species would have been destroyed by loggers before now.

Long ago, heavy snowfall split in two the arbutus beside our cabin. Next spring we discovered on the ground a three-forked chunk, a symmetrical tripod. I used it as legs for a table, the top a polished cedar burl. That was my most satisfactory wood-work. I never saw its like.

To build my office, it was regrettable but necessary to fell an arbutus of a foot's girth. As my handsaw approached the centre of the trunk I heard steel grating on some hard substance. So I withdrew the saw, chopped with an axe and found at the tree's heart a stone about four inches in diameter. How it got there we could not guess.

While the forest panted and struggled in drought, I was nei-ther idle nor lacking expert advice. Allan Gropp, my yellow-bearded and pot-bellied friend from across the lake, who en-joyed a high reputation as a craftsman of wood, a cabinetmaker of distinguished talent, faithfully observed my poor efforts. They never satisfied him. His criticism was constructive and kindly but firm. The mortise and tenon joints of my furniture, he intimated, were imperfect. "When I make a joint," he added, "you can't put a razor blade into the crack." Gropp would go away, shaking his head.

No one had seen him make a joint or lift a tool, and when the steps of his cabin rotted, I had to replace them. He watched me work, frequently interrupting with useful suggestions, but though he made no protest aloud I knew that he was dissatisfied with the result.

(According to local legendry, Gropp was once informed that Joe McGillicuddy had caught the largest rainbow trout ever known on the lake. Where, asked Gropp, had McGillicuddy been fishing? Told that the rainbow came from the West Arm, Gropp exclaimed: "The silly fool! He should have fished off Hunters' Point.")

Under Gropp's voluntary superintendence, the work of our camp proceeded and even involved the young generation. In-evitably the kids of the neighbourhood decided to build a tree house. I took no part in their enterprise, but Gropp never tired of instructing the builders in architectural design.

When one of them fell about ten feet and broke his arm, I was not surprised and soon had him in hospital at Duncan, where the bone was quickly set. The craftsman of wood explained to the boy that he should not have stepped on a loose plank.

To me Gropp predicted that most or all the boys would come to a bad end in their mature lives. But he did not himself live long enough to know the leading brain surgeon, judge, professor of economics and two geographers who had fashioned the tree house. They are now scattered, while their edifice, though sagging and falling apart, remains. I lack the energy to tear it down. Another generation must do that job.

Through all those happy years I had learned something—not much—about the forest's collective routine. In my time its growth from season to season looked slow, but it was steady and unmistakable. Firs and pines I had known as seedlings now towered above the cabin. Other trees, already massive when I arrived, were falling as the forest thinned itself.

Any space opened by their fall was immediately pre-empted by deciduous successors. Maples sprang up overnight and spread their jagged leaves to the sun like supplicating hands. From damp earth around the swamp, alders emerged in sudden thickets and after a few years displayed their white-mottled bark, apparently the work of a human artist.

These were minor events in a production vast, complex and immeasurable. The forest was moving towards its climax or its ruin, and mankind could not escape one of the two alternatives.

Perhaps seven or eight centuries ago, the naturalists speculate, Vancouver Island lay under a coniferous blanket, most of it hemlock, cedar and balsam that reproduced themselves in shade as Douglas-fir cannot do. When a mighty conflagration swept the Island's eastern half and opened it to the sun, the firs sprouted in myriads to create one of a future Canada's primary assets, now tragically depleted. But west of the Island's spine, on the Pacific rim with its drenching rain and ocean mists, fire was hardly known.

Today, driving over the mountain summit, you see a western forest quite different from its eastern neighbour appear within a mile or two. Down to the seashore, hemlock, cedar and gigantic spruce have already achieved a natural climax.

To the sensitive eye their many dead and crooked trees are depressing, in some places terrifying. No words can hint at the spectacle of the true rain forest. No man dropped into its dark welter could crawl out. No Indians of olden times came near it. Only devouring vegetable life seems to exist here.

It is observed safely enough nowadays from a plank catwalk built by the National Park authorities and, at some points, anchored to fallen cedars or spruce fifteen feet thick.

Compared to this turmoil and apparent chaos, with its own secret order, the second-growth forest east of the summit, even the few pathetic surviving patches of the original, like the famous grove beside Cameron Lake, seem friendly to man. Of course they are not, and man's invasion will make sure that climax is never reached except, perhaps, in some park reserves, centuries hence.

Canada is trying, very late and not fast enough, to replant its forest lands, but in many countries devastation is unrestricted, its effects on climate and mankind's vital oxygen supply ignored. As if this folly were harmless, the sickening vapours of industry are polluting, and in some countries killing, forests yet uncut.

No measurable acid rain has yet fallen on Vancouver Island, but doubtless that token of progress will appear in due course to broach a mixed practical and moral question—whether our species, if it avoids nuclear war, has the sense to maintain its brittle civilization, and whether it is justified in destroying other species wholesale before it, too, is self-destroyed without war. In a universe of laws and punishments, have forests no right to grow, rivers to flow unpolluted, animals to thrive and birds to sing, except by man's gracious consent?

In youth and middle age, I spent no time on such questions that had yet to be publicly asked. But I watched the symmetrical infant firs growing in the open spaces, the seedlings of feathery hemlock and flat-needled balsam robust in the shade. They were striving for climax but probably would never reach it.

All members of the forest community are imperilled by drought and its accomplice, fire. Every day we expected to see smoke on the far horizon. Instead, it appeared close to us on the flank of Mount Malahat, just below the railway tracks, immediately after the morning train had passed. Some passenger had

tossed a cigarette butt through the open window, the underbrush exploded, and within minutes the smaller trees were
aflame, fanned by a hot south wind.

The whole neighbourhood turned out to fight the fire with
shovels, axes and mattocks. We fought it all day and through
the night, but without the pumping engine and mile-long hose
of the volunteer village fire department, nothing could have
saved the forest down to the lakeshore.

Another old man and I patrolled the field below the mountain, using wet sacks to quench the spot fires in the dry grass,
while the young men struggled to keep the hose in front of the
advancing flames and the women served us with coffee and
sandwiches.

Despite our clumsy efforts, we might well have failed if the
railway had not rushed tank cars from Victoria and, at sunrise,
deluged the hillside. As Wellington said of Waterloo, our little
victory was a damned close run thing.

In the next summer the forest's repair began. Living roots
stitched up the ravelled earth before it could slide down the hill.
The first green appeared in creeping blackberry vines. Then
came the pink of fireweed and cautious shoots of ferns, willows
and maples.

The interlaced mesh that protects the underground fabric was
largely rewoven by the following year. Deciduous trees stood
half a foot high, some arbutus stumps thrust out glossy twigs,
and now we found a few bold seedlings of fir, each with a reddish bead, like a pale garnet, on its tip. The forest had taken hold
again.

This recovery seemed improbable in the year of our worst
drought. But the weather changed right after the fire. The
barometer suddenly fell and pointed to storm. The air turned
sultry and oppressive. Even crude human senses felt the electricity in it.

At dusk, lightning streaked the western sky and we heard the
first faint rumble of distant thunder. Its sound rose as the storm
moved towards us. By midnight, lightning danced on the hills
around the lake and struck, with deafening crash, along the
shore. A dozen fires broke out. Just when we expected a disaster

that no human agency could repel, the black sky opened. Raindrops bounced off the lake's flat surface as if propelled from below. Most of Vancouver Island was safely soaked before dawn.

Now we saw the countryside transformed, and we breathed the clean, fresh odour of wet, steaming earth. The forest drank deep, its pumps working overtime. The ferns brandished their swords again, the limp brush revived, the slugs, long hidden in dark crannies, emerged in shiny new uniforms of green. Underfoot the paths ceased to crackle and oozed moisture. Deer and raccoons approached the lake in silence. Invisible to us, the bacteria must have resumed their labours.

Relief from drought, though a blessed event, always demands a price in camp. No freak of climate but a law of nature draws guests here when a rainy spell begins. They are the victims of a peculiar Canadian madness.

In the August days of high summer, the nation's roads can barely contain the human lemmings who flee from their cities built at infinite cost to cottages built of cardboard and a wild surmise. That flight never lacks its infuriating and laughable misadventures. Invariably the beer or the family cat is left behind and must be rescued by a return trip to town. A couple of the kids become carsick and relieve their stomachs beside the road. The expensive bucket of ice cream has melted. So have the driver and his wife. Tempers are short, conversation sharp. Domestic harmony is the first casualty of the escape to paradise. And the rain keeps falling.

In the meantime we await the onslaught, our sense of hospitality at a low ebb, our normal compassion shrivelling. But the experienced camper has learned to greet visitors with an air of jollity that deceives nobody. The rain, he says, will soon stop and the sun will shine. The most ignorant guest knows the host is lying.

On this hideous weekend what else can he do? For him there are fixed rules of hosthood, for the visitors no code of guesthood, and they are quickly bored.

In the average camp like ours certain entertainment is provided. We have shelves of paperback detective stories, but since the last pages are generally missing the murderer is seldom discovered. A tattered copy of *Hamlet* and a classic work on mediaeval laws of primogeniture fail to amuse the ordinary reader. Bridge or cribbage games tend to be complicated because the winter rats have eaten the ace of spades, or was it the nine of diamonds? Our jigsaw puzzles have all been mixed together and after a few hours of frustration are abandoned.

Still the rain beats down and the roof begins to leak. Pails are distributed at strategic points. The fireplace smokes. The oven of the kitchen stove cannot be heated sufficiently to cook the roast. The kids swim from the wharf, return to the cabin in wet bathing suits and leave extra puddles on the floor. The host's grin is fading, his laugh rather hollow.

By another law of nature the company always includes a corpulent lady of uncertain age. She reclines on the couch, sipping a tumbler of colourless liquid that may be water or may not. She watches the rain, mutters to herself and then, of a sudden, emits a piercing shriek and demands immediate transportation to the city.

Her hysteria is cured by more glasses of colourless liquid, and she snores gently. The other guests pass the time in lighthearted talk of nuclear war, planetary pollution and the ghastly blunders of all governments. The day seems endless, but finally everyone goes to bed and, oddly enough, nobody catches pneumonia in the damp blankets.

At last the weekend passes. The guests are profuse in thanks for their glimpse of the real wilderness as seen through the windows. An hour after they have driven away an unalterable law of nature brings the sun out again.

Concerning such affairs much nonsense has been printed.

It is said, for instance, that crafty hosts pretend they are exhausted and close to collapse, in the vague hope of assistance. This attempt to shame guests into labour has never been practised in our camp. Nor has the Tom Sawyer method of exhibiting simple jobs as too complex for laymen and therefore enviable.

The last thing I ever wanted was help from well-meaning city dudes who blunt precious double-bitted axes on rocks, break handles, twist saw blades and carry to the kitchen wet wood piled in the shed to dry for next year's use.

Avoiding such risks, I tried to divert guests by explaining the brand-new inventions that make camp life so easy—the apparatus for cooking food without electricity and burning fuel supplied gratis whenever you cut it, the lamps consuming a substance known as coal oil if the power line fails, the vehicle moving on one wheel, transporting huge loads and requiring no labour but the muscles of the owner who pushes it over a rough trail.

As I informed the guests, a man rising at dawn, lighting the stove, replenishing the woodbox, sawing a few logs, mending a leaky roof and decayed bridge, making furniture, painting the verandah, cementing some fractured stone walls and clearing a blocked drain will enjoy the whole day until twilight and be healthy and wise, though seldom wealthy.

All this was the harmless persiflage of an old camp man, and sometimes it was actually believed. I had known many seasons of sun and rain, much happiness, solitude and good friends long gone across the wooden bridge. In truth I welcomed company and looked forward to urban life with horror.

The high summer of August waned too soon. Already the first gilded maple leaves had dropped along the trail. The mountainside had turned amber, the kinnikinnic berries red, the dawn air crisp. We could no longer deny these old signals. Autumn was on the way.

Canada's
Own Season

NO DOUBT AUTUMN of some sort comes to other lands, but it has belonged especially to Canada by unwritten title and historic squatters' rights ever since the first settlers at Quebec, twenty-eight Frenchmen, watched the last ship float down the St. Lawrence and leave them alone on an unmapped continent where starvation and scurvy would kill more than half of them before spring.

Nowadays, Canadians are protected from such misery, and by mid-September autumn's radiance penetrates the dullest among us. Nothing can dilute its colour, sound and scent. Nothing changes its pungency, bittersweet. No adjective in the language describes it and none is needed when all Canadians see it with their eyes, smell it with their noses and feel its rough male kiss. The clock tells us that the days are dwindling as the planet's northern flank turns southward on the smooth autumnal hinge. The thermometer records the drop in summer's heat, and we know, by a sixth sense, that, like the year, our lives are winding down.

English poets did their best to paint autumn from the limited palette of words. They produced great literature, but Keats's female figure dozing on a granary floor, tipsy with hard cider and poppy fumes, is not the autumn of Canada. Nor do Canadians cower and bleed, like Shelley, in his wild west wind even if their own wind can be wild enough to shake town and wilderness. Few Canadians share Tennyson's idle tears while looking on the happy autumn fields and remembering the days that were no more.

To Dot and me the yellow fields of the Rogers farm brought a different message, and the season itself differs widely from coast to coast. Between the Maritimes and the Great Lakes, the eastern forest blazes in chilly conflagration, and the smoke of leaf fires perfumes the city streets. The prairies are gilded with stubble. Poplars spread their bullion across the Rockies for thousands of miles, each leaf fluttering and falling like a gold coin. The huge foliage of the Pacific coast maple turns gold, too, and the little vine maple and the dogwood crimson.

At this time of year our living was easy, our diet replete with corn, tomatoes, lettuce, beans, squash, cauliflowers, a second crop of tender young carrots and, until the neighbourhood was populated and small boys discovered our orchard, brimming with apples, pears and plums. We gathered the fruit, hung braided onions from the basement ceiling, filled the potato bin and kept the squash at the temperature prescribed in the garden books.

It wasn't much of a harvest when Canada reaped grain and stored other foodstuffs in millions of bushels, and cattle fattened on the bunch grass of the Alberta foothills and the Cariboo ranges. Still, we enjoyed a figment of independence. Come what might, we would be nourished until spring.

Our imagined security was hard to maintain after the road at the bottom of the hill had been widened and paved to serve the noisy traffic, and kids from the new subdivisions walked or bicycled through our meadow as a short cut to school. Fortunately their invasion was still far ahead, even in our middle years.

A real harvest kept George Rogers busy. He had packed his barn loft with June hay and now was making ensilage. Long stalks of corn and big mangels grown in his wet lower field were shredded in a chopping machine and lifted on an endless belt to the top of his silo. For cows, this sweetish mixture would be a winter treat.

In our house an immemorial Canadian rite was faithfully observed. From the kitchen oozed the autumn fragrance long known to country women but, like the weather, indescribable. Pickling time had arrived.

My mother, mother-in-law and wife each followed her separate recipe in friendly competition of ripe tomatoes, green tomatoes, onions, cucumbers, cauliflowers, peppers and what else I never asked. Soon pickles and jams filled the basement shelves. Today's young working wives buy good products in the shops, but their houses cannot know the distilled essence of autumn.

It even seemed to restore Rawling's damaged sense of taste. Dot always sent him home with bottled treasures.

"Ooh, ooh!" he'd wheeze. "Pickles! Jam! Ambrosia for the gods and much too good for 'em."

He particularly relished our plums and would eat a dozen of them off the trees. But he was choosy about our apples, deploring the lack of English pippins, with their superior tang, and he often warned Dot against a common household error.

"Never debase apples in sauce," he said. "No, no, just stew 'em and leave the skins on or you'll lose all the goodness."

When he went home to Vancouver, his valise heavily loaded with apples, he must have enjoyed an orgy of stew in his apartment beside English Bay.

One day he came to our place in a state of highest dudgeon. On a Vancouver street he had encountered his old enemy from a bitter editorial dispute—A. M. Manson, former attorney general of British Columbia and now a member of its Supreme Court. "You know what that fellow did?" Rawling sputtered. "Why, he spoke to me! Imagine it! By God, he stopped and spoke to me!" Though we couldn't imagine it, Rawling never forgave that outrage.

Apart from its edible produce, autumn was also the time of the year's late blooms. Dahlias, chrysanthemums, lingering nasturtiums and the final gorgeous flowering of roses prolonged for a little while the look of summer when most of Canada's gardens had been frozen.

Dot preserved clusters of hydrangeas, Chinese lanterns and the pods of honesty or silver dollars, to deck the house until heather, jasmine, snowdrop and crocus time early in the new year.

By autumn the growth of a garden neglected during our absence in camp had blocked the ground-floor windows of the town house, and new pyracantha shoots, twelve feet long, equipped with piercing thorns, had climbed above roof level. My hands, though encased in thick leather gloves, were always stabbed by these hidden spears as I cut them back.

Ivy that I should never have planted in the beginning had crawled up the chimney and the oak trees, seeded itself in the rockery and, left alone, would have covered the whole garden. Everywhere weeds flourished in rank luxuriance. It took me weeks to fight down all these prolific aggressors.

In a year of ceaseless rain, fortunately never repeated, our potatoes rotted under the blight that once starved the Irish people. In another year of drought caterpillars and mysterious spores denuded our fruit trees. By the vagaries of the weather or the natural injustice of life, Harry Snape was spared such evils and took all the credit for his luck.

Now a skilled and arrogant grower, he exhibited his vegetable marrows of enormous size in the fall fair at Saanichton. After winning several prizes he intimated, none too subtly, that his specimens, four times as large as mine, were the result of closer attention, scientific fertilization and an Englishman's native horticultural instinct.

His success, reported with other news of the fair in the Victoria papers, and his monthly old-age pension from Ottawa had reconciled him at last to Canada. He no longer talked of returning to England and, instead, was meditating his candidacy for membership in the Saanich Council.

"Wot the country needs," he informed me privately, "is leaders, men with idears." He had many idears, to be disclosed at the proper time. Meanwhile he borrowed one of my Canadian history books and may even have read or skimmed it. But after calm second thoughts, he decided not to seek municipal office because it would involve him in politics, which, as a soldier, he despised.

It happened that our neighbourhood had suddenly become, at this time, a focal point in British Columbia's public affairs. Preparing for their party's leadership convention, the Saanich Conservatives met in the Lake Hill community hall to elect their delegates. In a dispute of high principle, half the audience walked out and, under a street light, appointed its own delegation led by a man named Stubbs, whose slogan, "Stubbs is stubborn," became the rebels' call to arms.

Two separate groups then appeared at the stalemated Kamloops convention, and each demanded official status. The votes of either were judged sufficient to decide the choice of a new leader and probably the next provincial election. The Battle of Lake Hill, as the newspapers called it, was long, angry and confused until the convention drafted Dr. Simon Fraser Tolmie, a member of Parliament, a native of Saanich and the son of pioneers, who tried desperately but failed to reject the leadership. We regarded the result of this historic affair and the subsequent Conservative victory as our local contribution to major politics.

But it confirmed Snape's disgust. Nothing like this, he said, could happen in England or even India. He would have nothing to do with such hanky-panky. Besides, his marrows, his brood of white Leghorn chickens and his explosive home-brewed beer required all his time and compensated him, in part anyhow, for the scarcity of pheasants.

The illegal shotgun was seen in the neighbourhood no more. Without realizing his fate, Snape had almost become a Canadian.

The same process, over a longer time, had slowly transformed Rawling, once the very portrait of John Bull. At the age of sixty-five, he retired from the Vancouver *Province* and bought a newly built cottage some fifteen miles north of us on the shore of Saanich Inlet. He also acquired an automobile and constantly endangered his life while driving it to the common danger.

In his lonely retreat, after the fraternity of a metropolitan newspaper, he welcomed visitors. Having planted half a dozen young apple trees (pippins, of course), he didn't trust himself to prune them.

"I've no genius for gardening," he explained, so I did the pruning job. In payment he regaled Dot and me with thick beef-steaks or greasy chump chops of mutton, his innocent pride, topped by hot rum rations mixed with lime juice and butter. Somehow we survived his hospitality.

On these occasions, his tongue loosened by the rations, he discussed at length his favourite cabbages and kings, most emphatically the virtues of conservatism and the hazards of liberalism in government.

"Any man above fifty years of age," he declared, "is a Tory or a bloody fool. But the silly old politicians don't know their silly old business."

His solitude was not to last long. By sawing firewood on the beach and lugging it up to the cottage, he strained his heart. The doctors insisted that he move to town where they could look after him. Protesting but finally accepting their advice, he sold his cottage, gave away his handmade furniture—some of the best pieces to us—rented a room in the Union Club, drank his rum rations with similar lonely men and wrote vagrant columns for the *Province*. Though he was comfortable in the club, he had relinquished his independence, and his reliance on others sorely vexed him. He frequently drove at reckless speed to our place.

For the time being, our lives were unshadowed and the nation seemed to face no dangerous threats. How unbelievably it had changed since the first Frenchmen settled on the banks of the St. Lawrence. How fortunate were their successors, the people of modern Canada, most fortunate on earth, we thought, by rightful measurement. And yet, as we realized in later years, the march of progress had stumbled everywhere.

The Quebec garrison could count on a ship arriving next spring with life's necessities and carrying no missiles designed for death. They could count on land, water and air free of poisons, on outer space uncrowded by satellites and the nuclear weapons of Star Wars. But we of the contemporary world cannot count on tomorrow's news, the sanity of the superpowers or the survival of human life on a tormented minor planet. Ours is called the age of science and enlightenment. In fact it is the age of mystery and menace, unlike any past age.

Even Dot and I, in our little lives, had come far from ancient stone houses in Ontario, the flaming Laurentian forest and the age of Canada's innocence. Like the nation, we were fortunate. Autumn fields brought us no tears of wild regret. We could not know it then, but they were only postponed for later shedding.

The Dwindling Days

SOMETIMES AUTUMN will come late in the forest, straining on summer's traces. Hot days may continue all through September. But three months after the June solstice the sun's declining meridian is marked by the most casual eye. The play of slanting sunlight on the gnarled firs, the webbed bark of the cedars and silken boles of the arbutus, behind them gulfs of shadow daubed here and there by the yellow of maple leaves just before they fall, paint a picture seen only in autumn.

A whimsical lake changes its mood and deepens its colours from gunmetal to jade to sapphire. Its haze, in ghostly dance at sunrise, will soon burn off. Then the water is so calm that it reflects like a polished mirror the shoreline, the individual trees, the cabins, boats and sky—a double world, half of it turned upside-down.

In a different mood, the surface is ruffled, but smooth patches remain, streaked with the pink of dawn, until the north wind blows, churning up whitecaps and reminding us of storms to come. For the time being the wind drops towards evening. Moon and stars float and multiply on the gentle wavelets of still autumn nights.

Already the birds feel the seasonal shift. Above the water, swallows devour flying insects. A lone osprey wheels, dives and emerges with a fish in its talons. But the mallard ducks look restless, swooping up and down the lake at random as they prepare for escape to the south. Some of the Canada geese will live here all winter unless the lake freezes solid—a rare occurrence. The first chickadees, juncos and cobalt-blue Steller's jays have arrived from northern regions. Even a varied thrush has come out of the mountains, long before its usual time, perhaps foreseeing an early cold snap.

Without intelligence (as humans know it) the forest, too, prepares for winter.

Beneath the giants, crimson hips dangle from the wild rose bushes, purple berries from the salal and Oregon grape. Since we last visited them months ago, the infant jack pines in the field have almost doubled their height. From the ground we cannot see the growth of the big firs, cedars, hemlocks and balsams. At their age it is slow, hardly measurable. In the tranquil dusk they stand motionless, the year's work apparently finished. But while the sap is falling, the roots will not cease to spread. The western forest knows no repose, only brief intervals of silence. But in the east, beside Walden Pond, Henry Thoreau heard the silence broken by a musical hum "as distant as a hive in May," and he liked to imagine that it was the sound of trees muttering their secret thoughts.

Thoreau was a genius whose own thoughts became literary classics. We could find no words for our trees and in windless autumn weather detected no hum. But the slightest breeze started the forest whispering, and not long afterwards it would be moaning, howling, booming and creaking in winter tempest.

At all seasons its appetite for territory was gluttonous. A settler clears a few acres, builds a hut of shakes and then moves away. If he returns a decade later he finds no clearing. Alders have taken possession of the damp earth, firs and pines of the dry. The hut has collapsed but the shake roof, made of durable cedar, is not yet rotten and lies flat on the ground. When a retired couple builds a sound house, the garden must not be neglected for a single year, or rank trespassers will choke it.

Three years after fire had seared it, the hill above the lake was covered by a thin layer of blackberry vines, white daisies, name-less weeds, bracken and green shoots from the charred stumps of maple and willow.

All over the Pacific shelf that scene is endlessly repeated as on a mouldering, overworked palimpsest. Everywhere the jungle is on the march, ready to strike at the first opening in the defence line of its archenemy, man. But even without him it re-mains vulnerable to the other enemies of insect life and wind-carried disease.

Observing it in autumn, we never knew which healthy-looking trees, like some vigorous human friends, would die be-fore we returned in the spring. After one unforgettable winter we found that a local tornado had cut a gash a hundred yards long straight through a grove of virgin firs. They lay uprooted in a dense tangle of branches. We needed the next winter to burn the slash and three summers to saw the trunks and lug the wood, piece by piece, to the nearest trail. Within five years, maples and alder, thirty feet high, were crowding the gash and elbowing each other for sunlight. But they would be pushed aside later on by evergreens, now mere seedlings.

Into such autumnal realities strode the phantom figure of Archie, born by immaculate conception on my typewriter. Still, his origin had a certain legitimacy since he was modelled on the man of all forest crafts whose broadaxe had shaped the heavy beams for our rebuilt cabin. Archie was not as good a man as his prototype. I endowed him with a strain of guile, a thirst for strong drink and a chest-length beard, but he was good enough for my newspaper columns and gradually took on almost be-lievable life of his own.

Even Rawling approved of him as a fiction truer than fact. "But then," he wrote from his roost in the Victoria club, "we all live by myths, not facts. There's more truth in the wildest fairy tale than in any encyclopaedia or government blue book. Go ahead, quote Archie as you please, and he'll make more sense than you do."

Rawling let his imagination soar in a long postscript: "Archie can wear a variety of disguises. He may be a ruined millionaire hiding from his creditors, a bank robber escaped from jail, the

Duke of Kakiak incognito or the exiled prince of Ruritania. On the other hand, he may not. Take your choice.

"If you ever read a book," the letter concluded, "you'd know what G. K. Chesterton said about facts. In one of his essays I find that he refused to surrender 'a total and frequent experience of a poem to a false re-encounter with the actual lines.' That's the meat of it in poetry or prose. Never mind the facts. They only get in the way of the truth. And remember something else from G. K. He doubted whether any truth could be told except in parable. Archie is nothing but a parable. So are you. So are all of us."

Archie, like his honest progenitor, served me well. In print I was always paying him (generally with alcoholic beverages) for odd jobs about the camp. In reality he helped to pay its expenses by providing ideas for newspaper trivia.

His reports of society in the village seemed to amuse the public, and all of them had a factual origin. That was true, even if carefully disguised, of Bill McGillicuddy's extramarital adventures and his notorious affair with the blonde waitress in the Duncan hamburger joint. Still more accurate was Archie's candid description of the bachelors' party on New Year's Eve, which contributed handsomely to the revenue of the government liquor store and left the guests horizontal, somewhat damaged but sleeping peacefully at dawn.

More serious village news concerned the performance of *Hamlet* by the amateur dramatic troupe. According to Archie, it was a notable success, though the plot confused him. He informed us, "You can't keep track of all those killers with the funny names. Everybody kills everybody else in the last act on account of murder runs through the whole Hamlet family. Begonia Clutterbuck, the old-maid school teacher from England, says Shakespeare was quite a clever guy and wrote some pretty good stuff, but you need a dictionary to know what he means. Not much, I guess."

In all his letters to us, Archie emphasized the drought afflicting him and his comrades in seasons of teeming rain. Only liquid contributions from town could relieve the victims of unnatural disaster. But Archie professed undying contempt for all summer dudes, as he called us, looked forward with horror to our return and yearned for the healing solitude of winter. "Then," he said, "a man can breathe again. God, how I dread the spring!"

Archie's gossip was not his main value in my job. I made him utter outrageous political heresies that I was too cowardly to acknowledge directly. Of course no reader was deceived by such an obvious pretence, but no politician could answer a phantom without making a fool of himself. Thus secure and apparently well informed about public affairs, Archie continued his insult for many years and often relieved me from spells of newspaper drought.

There was nothing original or new about this arrangement. Long ago the first great Canadian humorist, Judge T. C. Haliburton, invented Sam Slick, the immortal clockmaker, to lampoon the society of Nova Scotia. My phantom, alas, was neither slick nor immortal, only outrageous.

The autumn reality was more vivid than his prose. At sunset the forest stood in stark profile, each tree distinctly etched against the blood-red sky. Now we knew that the Group of Seven, painting an eastern landscape, had not exaggerated the colours of Canada. After the western colours faded and a harvest moon like a round of ripe cheddar hung over the mountains, we often walked on the road when traffic had paused and darkness worked its sorcery.

In daylight the scars of human presence disfigured nature's work. Highway crews with their travelling derricks and mechanical saws had slashed the trees close to the power line. Telephone poles stood in ugly nakedness. Decaying shacks and even new houses seemed ugly, too. But moonlight blurred these shapes, melted the buildings into the forest and expunged the scars as if a film of silver had been poured over everything.

When we reached a bend in the road and the moon was hidden by the hill, the stars swam out to confront us with the beauty or the horror of the universe. Beholding glimmers from distance unimaginable, the emptiest mind is jolted into thought and the greatest member of humankind becomes less than the fraction of an atom.

Thus every human must face the paramount question and judge that the universe has some meaning or that it is a chemical accident, perhaps a grisly joke. If the question is evaded, life's voyage may be comfortable but it will lack compass, ballast or anchor. So Lincoln judged when he said that a reasonable man, looking down on our planet from another, might well be an atheist. However, it was impossible for Lincoln to conceive that a man looking upward from the earth would see no evidence of an intelligent cosmic purpose.

We also had reached the same judgement, without the means to express it, but the spangled vault above us looked as frightening as it was grand. Weak creatures, we groped our way home along the pitch-black trail, saw the light in our kitchen window and, like our ancestors from remote ages, sought the imagined safety of the cabin as they sought it in their caves.

A flimsy roof could not muffle the message of the stars, and yet all the apparatus of modern societies, though it has mastered space travel, is designed to shut out the menace of the void. The more affluent and sophisticated the society the more insulation, the thicker mental carapace, it builds around itself until the fortunate people of the Western countries huddle beside an electronic screen and drug themselves with technicoloured fairy tales.

We had no television set, the cabin was uninsulated and soon, in annual disorder, we must retreat from the forest to the edge of the town.

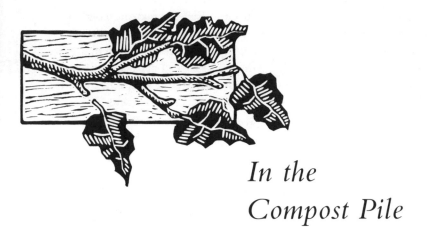

In the
Compost Pile

THE FAIR-WEATHER FRIENDS of the outdoors suffer a psychic trauma when, in brown October, they return to civilization, exhausted by months of supposed idleness. But for us the trauma is brief. With our strong moral fibre we soon accustom ourselves to urban hardships. Victuals, we rediscover, can be cooked electrically, without the need to stoke a woodstove. Electricity also provides hot water in limitless volume. An oil furnace automatically warms a house on cool mornings.

After a week or so we learn to live with these implements of decadence. We almost begin to accept as fact the bogus security of streets. We rely on our burglar alarm, the police, the fire department and the friendly neighbours. The bogus peasants find creature comforts becoming tolerable.

From Emily Carr's grim wilderness we have moved to the soft pastoral scenery of John Constable, two separate worlds. But in forest and field alike, if the weather is fair, October's sunset exposes the same vermilion disc behind the vertical evergreens or the crooked arms and the feathery plumes of the oaks. Without leaving home or paying an admission charge, we briefly glimpse nature's rose window, finer than any in cathedrals built by man.

Throughout Canada, the year's tenth month wears diverse

motley. Climate, colour and human affairs are so varied that a foreigner might think he had travelled different nations.

On the Pacific coast, flowers still bloom as if warm days would never cease. The sharp dawn air turns balmy, and sometimes hot, at noon to caress the skin like silk raiment. Inland only a hundred miles, frost has already effaced the garden's splendour. Snow is falling on the prairies. Householders are installing storm windows, women taking fur coats from storage, kids retrieving forgotten skates and hockey sticks.

As a rule October is genial, but we all know, even on the rim of the Japan Current, when autumn is dying. Our native mists and mellow fruitfulness are tempered by the first portents of winter in a northern land.

After a touch of frost, a preliminary hint of the season ahead, our vegetable garden becomes a ruin, almost an eyesore. Squash, marrow and cucumber plants sprawl flat and dead on the ground. Vines of tomatoes and beans cling, shrivelled, to their stakes. Dry corn stalks rattle in the wind. But frost improves the flavour of parsnips, and the sturdy leeks. Perhaps even some carrots and cabbages will survive the winter if it is mild.

To clear up the annual wreckage is no minor task, and it grew harder year by year. When I could afford their modest wages, a curious procession of jobbing gardeners helped me from time to time.

One of them, a happy-go-lucky youngster and high school dropout, joined the Canadian Air Force as soon as the second war began. A couple of years later we learned that, as a bomber pilot, he had been shot down somewhere in Germany.

Next came a morose and silent Englishman, older than I, with a hairless head shaped like an egg, small end up. He said he had long worked on the farms of Surrey, but his aversion to work of any form led to his early resignation. Through mysterious influences he was employed by the municipal garbage department, a sinecure as he judged it.

A hulking fellow named Ramage followed him to our place. Ramage, whose vast beard seemed to be fashioned of copper wire, spent most of his time leaning on a shovel, wrapt in meditation. But his time, and my money, had not been squandered.

One day, after digging lightly and meditating heavily for several hours, Ramage informed me that we must part.

"I'm going in for a literary career," he said. "Writin' books and all. I've got a gift that way and I seen in the papers where a guy in Chicago teaches you by mail, only ten bucks a lesson. It's easy, he says, a piece of cake, when you get the hang of it. And the pay is good."

With his wages, his literary gift, my congratulations (and private relief), he took the bus to town and, I hoped, to fame. We never heard of him again.

Now the perfect helper appeared from nowhere. Jimmy, as everyone called him, was then hardly more than a boy, and today, after our collaboration of some forty years, I cannot think of him as old.

In that time he did not once fail to start work in our garden at eight o'clock each Thursday morning, sunshine, rain or snow. He was small of stature, but as he aged his muscles seemed to lose none of their original strength. Though his education had been limited, his lined, quizzical face bespoke a fund of natural wisdom. Despite our opposite experience in life, we had known similar grief and became close friends. No friend of mine, however distinguished, was more honest and, in a wonderfully wild fashion, more humorous. And I knew no gardener who could dig, hoe and prune as much in one day.

Over midmorning coffee and cookies, Jimmy, an ardent sports fan, would discuss the latest news of baseball, football and hockey. He always punctuated our weekly exchange with astounding contortions of the English language. He told me, for example, that my cabbage seedlings "have been succumbed and disintegrated." Canadian politics, he said, needed more "equility."

The cookies were often "atrociously good," some of my observations "sensological" but others "dubistical," not to say "subnoxious" when I was "connivering" among politicians. He would never disclose his own political views and turned off questions on that subject with a sly grin. But he forgave my printed mistakes in the newspapers because "we're all under the mandate of eternal damnification."

How he managed to twist the conventional idiom so regularly and outrageously we did not learn for many years— possibly, we guessed, by reading the dictionary in his spare time. At last we learned that his word-hobby was more complicated than we had supposed. He finally broke down and confessed that, listening to his portable radio and the talk of his employers in town, he lumped their words together and invented new ones. To what end?

"Well," said Jimmy, "it makes folks laugh a little. It's what you call a contribution, eh?" Pausing at the kitchen door, he added: "The Lord protect you till we meet again." We met as usual next Thursday.

For him our garden, with others, was a source of low but sufficient income. For us it was a dependant, like a child or a dog. The more attention we gave it, the more it demanded. We were its slaves.

After months of neglect, its demands, in late autumn, seemed exorbitant, and already it displayed the first intimations of spring.

Heather buds promised blossom at Christmas. The fine green sprouts of grape hyacinth had broken through the surface of the earth. Snowdrops soon followed. Digging the flower beds, we turned up daffodil bulbs and the brown corms of crocus. They, too, were sprouting, while nearby so-called autumn crocuses (that belong to an entirely different species) brandished their coral chalices as if they had misread the calendar.

Among the background shrubs we found that seedlings of maple, dogwood and cedar had established themselves and had to be ruthlessly exterminated. The pyracantha we cut back a few weeks earlier had reacted to our assault by thrusting out new branches equipped with thorns as sharp as needles. We pruned again and our heap of brush to be burned in the winter kept rising. Bindweed, known as morning glory in a false euphemism, crawled up the fruit trees. Even detestable chemical sprays could not kill it nor a variety of campanula (planting it was my father's only grave mistake) that spread everywhere until we abandoned a hopeless struggle.

A gardener cannot afford too much benevolence. As in human affairs his choices are seldom satisfactory, more often second-best or dead wrong, and cannot be remedied.

To aggravate these problems, the kids of the new subdivisions had roamed our place all summer and left a spoor of gum wrappers, candy packages and, still worse, broken pop bottles. Collecting glass shards from under late-blooming dahlias, chrysanthemums and Michaelmas daisies, or out of the lily pools, was a mean chore.

We were irritated also by the young trespassers' habit of stirring up a big anthill that we had long watched in the process of construction. On our return from the woods in five successive years, we found the ants repairing their devastated home.

They swarmed through the ruins, each carrying a minute burden—a pine needle or a fragment of wood—to fill the holes left by the children. In a month or so, the job was finished, the mansion of conical design ready for winter and, no doubt, another season of vandalism.

Here a glaring allegory was legible. Humans could do almost anything if, like the ants, they worked together. Instead, unlike the ants, they failed to co-operate even to avoid the risk of nuclear suicide or the pollution of their little planet.

The neighbourhood vandals efficiently pilfered our apple crop, but in one memorable autumn they overlooked the first dozen fruits borne by a Northern Spy after its slow growth of a dozen years. The best of all Canadian apples, plump, rubicund and luscious, were baked, and they lived up to our high expectations.

A pair of trees planted in our young days produced more walnuts than we could gather with hands stained a durable brown for the next several weeks. The crows waited until the nuts fell and the green outer rind split. Then they seized the hard inner capsules and dropped them from a great height upon the paved lane to break the shells. Swooping down, they extracted and swallowed the tasty meat.

If the wind blew strongly, acorns fell on our roof with the clatter of a kettle drum, and we slithered on them along the garden paths as on ball bearings. By this time, infant oaks had sprung up, nearly a foot high, from last year's seeds in the rockery and perennial beds to become a nuisance. With a guilty feeling we uprooted them and ended lives that might otherwise have lasted for centuries.

Fallen horse chestnuts seldom germinated and were inedible, but their skins of burnished mahogany, pleasant to the touch, must fascinate all Canadian children. All youngsters of normal instinct hurl these pellets at one another and, in the old English game of conkers, each player swings the weapon on a cord to hit and crack their opponent's. In my latter years I would pick up the shiny globules, feel their smooth rinds and remember life before its troubles began.

A different and baneful crop appeared on the lawn after the first autumn rains. Fungi of many sorts, white, brown and yellow, emerged overnight and had to be quickly collected and burned or their roots, a spreading gossamer, would drain the soil of nutriment. Toadstools in a fairy ring (that charming name for a deadly menace) make a patch of lawn green in one season and kill it the next.

To exhume long fungus roots, you must dig deep and fill the hole with clean earth. This job recurred every year until we learned to fine-comb the lawn and remove the parasites by hand before they released their spores. Among the varied growths, some of our expert friends said, were excellent mushrooms and other edible treats. But we did not test such advice.

October, supposedly a time of ease for tired rustics, allowed us scant leisure.

Deciduous trees began to unload their burdens of foliage, and we had to rake and move them to our compost pile. The stately columns of the lombardy poplars had turned a pale lemon hue. The native maples donned luminous yellow and some imported varieties a brilliant crimson. An English hawthorn near our back door looked as red as any tree in the Laurentian forest. A thicket of wild cherries seemed to diffuse an orange nimbus while the dogwoods floated in vintage Burgundy. The oaks could offer no more than a dull russet tinge, but their leaves had a superior value.

All the deciduous trees were now engaged in the same complex process. At the tip of every twig a barrier of extra cells formed to cut off and jettison the attached leaf and prevent it from evaporating moisture that the tree would need when its sap-pumps slowed down for the season of cold. The silent power expended on these preparations, the final ripening of seeds and the rearrangement of molecules to paint the autumnal forest are beyond human measurement and imagination.

We could only ply our rakes in a task that seemed futile on windy days as leaves filled the air like a brown blizzard, heaped up windrows against the rock walls and clung to the shrubs.

In those busy days a trick learned from my father came in handy. If strangers halted in their walk down the lane to pass the time of day and question me about my work, I greeted them with an idiot's leer, pointed at my mouth to show that I was dumb, muttered gurgling sounds or shouted some remembered sentence of schoolboy Latin to indicate that I was a foreigner who spoke no English. The trick always worked. As the strangers hurried away, I often heard them protest that the Canadian government was admitting too many undesirable immigrants.

Leaf-raking looks simple and easy. In truth, it demands much strength and skill. My own experience with a miniature rake and wheelbarrow at the age of four had begun in the orchard of my grandparents' home in Prescott, Ontario. Now, though childhood and youth had long passed, the enchantment of leaves was renewed. My children and grandchildren jumped, as I had jumped, into the drifting heaps that rustled with the swish of wavelets on a sandy beach.

All this was a pleasing déjà vu, but we had work to do. In a wheelbarrow enlarged by a homemade wire rack, we moved the leaves to the compost pile, where bacteria, without further help from us or additives from the garden shops, completed the job. A multitude of hungry microorganisms settled down comfortably to produce, in a single year, a precious stuff that crumbled in our fingers and contained more plant nourishment than any chemical fertilizer. We worked it into the roots of acid-loving heathers, azaleas and rhododendrons. They feasted on this diet that cost us nothing but our physical exhaustion.

When the oaks had shed their summer dress, they looked to us like arthritic titans struggling painfully up Christmas Hill, but their crisp, serrated leaves provided the richest element in the compost. They had body, fibre and substance lacking in the leaves of other trees.

No leaf of any kind was ever wasted on our place while leaf fires burned on countless streets all over Canada, its basic wealth carelessly depleted. In a just society, we thought, such havoc would be a capital offense, the culprits burned with their victims. Yet it went ignored and unpunished, even in Victoria, a temple of tree worship.

A compost pile enriched by age, layer on layer, may conceal evidence of happier times. Long after she had left this world, I found, deep down in the pile, the china head of a doll that once belonged to my daughter. Then the shovel turned up a rusty toy locomotive mislaid by my son. An old man's memory is a dubious asset.

Fourscore years had brought many changes in my life, but nature's routine did not change. By late October, when all the leaves had fallen, the cotoneasters of several breeds, the prickly Berberis and the holly offered their florid berry crops for the pleasure of our eyes and the nutrition of the birds. Flocks of robins and starlings gorged on a free lunch. Cedar waxwings, ruby-crowned kinglets, house finches, their heads wine-coloured, towhees with reddish sides, and black-capped juncos came from their summering regions. Chickadees and house wrens hopped about the bushes with lively twitter. Woodpeckers, even the lordly pileated type, hammered dead trees for grubs, scorning the berries. Some of the visitors paused only a day or two before they flew southward, but a company of azure-tinted Steller's jays with hoarse, scolding voices, would stay here until spring.

Now daylight was shrinking fast, darkness growing longer,

the night air colder. Autumn had almost reached its end. And before real winter arrived, we had a final job to do in the forest and a mighty spectacle to observe, far away.

In the Woodshed

THE CLOSING of a summer camp is a melancholy and laborious affair, hard on muscle and mind alike. It becomes harder as the years pass (and few are left to the aged leaseholder who calls himself the owner).

Preparations for winter exhaust the strongest men, even the young ones. Slippery roofs must be swept clean of pine needles, the pump dismantled, water pipes drained, heavy mattresses hung up to foil the devouring rats, porches sheathed in tin to resist wind, rain and snow.

Only yesterday, it seems, we opened the camp. Where have spring and summer gone in swift passage, taking with them so many passengers who will not return? What good has the season accomplished here and in the great world?

Not much, but in earlier days we could flatter ourselves with the physical improvements around us. That satisfaction has faded, but even on life's downward slope I still plan for the next camp opening by filling the woodshed.

Like tobacco, drink and drugs, wood can be an incurable addiction, and it had long held me in its grip. According to local gossip, my secret woodpiles along the forest paths were uncounted, forgotten and decayed. Percy Rawling denounced me as a miser and alleged that I never gave my wife the best-quality wood for her kitchen stove. "She'd only burn it," I was quoted as saying. Percy spread the slander until Dot almost came to believe him.

The facts were rather different. I sawed and chopped trees wherever they fell, and in some years of storm we had an embarrassment of riches. But after a few calm winters our fuel supply ran so low that I harvested dead firs a couple of inches thick. In seasons of feast I dreaded famine, knowing that the stove would burn two cords a year and the fireplace two more if the weather was chilly. Once, in ultimate humiliation, I was forced to buy cedar slabs from a mill because I would not cut healthy trees.

Against the cycle of surplus and want, the woodshed is the only insurance. It is also a profound study in economics, one of Canada's oldest, most valuable institutions and, like the garden, a lovesome thing, God wot. It contains not just some fuel but nearly all that mankind has learned, so far, about civilized society.

If such truths escape the sophisticated visitor from town, they are well understood by the simple denizens of the forest. We remember that Canada was built with axe and saw before machinery reached the frontier and that the early settlers could not have survived without their store of dry wood. They tamed half a continent, won their individual freedom and learned to govern themselves by free elections. Of this achievement the woodshed stands as a vivid symbol.

Any woodsman is saddened to realize that most of the contemporary generation has never used a cross-cut saw, a sharp double-bitted axe to fell trees, a blunt axe for splitting or, if necessary, a maul and steel wedge. No wonder our society and the world entire are in a lamentable state.

The obsolete saw hanging in our woodshed is rusty, long idle, but in its time it cut many big trees, two men pulling the eight-foot blade with the rhythmical motion of a ballet dance. Nowadays a saw manipulated by human hands is a curiosity, a museum piece. Clamorous and efficient chainsaws dominate— and devastate—the woods.

City folk know little of these weighty matters, less about the contents of the woodshed and still less about its meaning. But within it, the philosophic mind detects more sense than the world's governments exhibit.

After all, what is the secret of a well-managed economic system? It is the husbanding of vital resources against the freaks of climate, the follies of powerful groups, the ups and downs of the market, the madness of war. In humble miniature, the woodshed represents this whole process.

Its lesson, learned by the Canadian pioneers, has yet to be relearned by their successors when governments pile up mountainous debts, interest costs derange national budgets and candidates win elections by promising obvious impossibilities. If, occasionally, our politicians turned from rhetoric to reality and grasped an axe instead of a debating point or photo opportunity much social damage might be avoided.

For those who can read its message, the woodshed rebukes such errors. Neatly piled (a high skill in itself), the contents, unlike all paper assets and printed money, are real wealth, an honest measure of value never diminished by the legal counterfeiting known as inflation. And when the chopper inspects the drying wood for next spring's fire, he must be a little surprised by his own morality. His work, his sweat, his muscle and ache have created that wealth, or at least preserved it. He has asked no wages and he has toiled while his guests revelled in summer idleness.

There is a darker side to the lesson of the woodshed. A moral chopper should ask himself what right he has to nature's generosity when multitudes of human beings are cold in winter and hungry in all seasons. A nice question, especially for Canadians who, possessing a transcontinental treasure, grossly mismanage it by defying the woodshed principle.

The moral question remains, and it has baffled philosophers of every faith since mankind left its caves—how much of nature's yield does any nation or individual deserve? What volume of wealth are we entitled to hoard for our own use in woodshed or written contract? Is a man obliged to share it with his fellows who will not or cannot work? Is he truly his brother's keeper, or a superior personage with obligations only to himself?

Even more baffling questions assail the conscientious chopper. What will happen to mankind and its so-called living standard if its real wealth is depleted by an exploding world population? How much plunder, combined with the lethal poisons of industry, can nature sustain? Who will refill the planetary woodshed? And can it ever be refilled, ever cleansed?

Vagrant reveries of this sort did not long distress me when I worked at a chopping block saved from a huge fir and now battered and cracked like its owner. The block would last my time and perhaps serve my grandsons for a few years when I no longer needed it.

While he was still able to drive his car (always to the common danger but, miraculously, without serious accident), Percy Rawling used to visit the camp at closing time. Each year, he was, or pretended to be, anxious about the bridge and its probable collapse in the winter snow. To his amazement (and perhaps his chagrin), the structure would be undamaged. But after his latest inspection, he repeated his annual warning: "You'll never make a carpenter, my boy, never learn construction."

This seemed a little unfair since, without help, I had shored up the roof of our main porch, replaced two rotting corner posts and the floor around them and built three little houses, none flawless but all sturdy.

They did not impress Rawling who, always the skilled carpenter, detected every flaw. On the other hand, he approved my chock-full shed and dilated at some length, over a rum ration, on the use of wood as a fuel.

In France, where he had sampled the local diet behind the trenches of the first war, the better chefs, he recalled, would roast chickens on a spit only with the firewood of apple trees, while geese required the wood of pears.

"Bloody nonsense, of course," said Percy. "But we don't taste meat roasted any more. Roast beef? Ha, it's baked in an oven. *Baked,* I tell you. Roasting ended with the stove. But we had an open fireplace in our house when I was a boy. The beef was well and truly roasted. Now you only get the good stuff at some bloody awful public barbecue. And oh, the difference!"

At this recollection his mouth visibly watered. And then he

remembered an observation by Thoreau, one of his favourite writers, albeit American. "Wood," he said, "warms you twice, first in the cutting and second in the burning. So keep your woodshed full when I'm gone."

Though he was getting old and shaky, he did not go from this world before he had driven his car, accompanied by Torchy Anderson, the legendary editor of the *Province,* over a rough road in the British Columbia interior. A sharp rock punctured the bottom of the gasoline tank. Torchy crawled under it, stopped the drip with his finger and managed, by a feat of contortion, to hand Percy a stick of chewing gum. Instructed to chew it, Percy, all the while cursing a vile American habit, obeyed, and a sticky substance was applied to the leak. Thus repaired, the car reached a village garage before the last drop of fuel ran out. But Percy never forgot the horror of that day.

"Gar," he told me privately, "it tasted like cheap perfume in a Spanish whorehouse."

Not long after the gum episode, Percy was writing a column for the *Province* in his room at the Union Club, when he slumped over his desk. Dot and I had lost not only a wise and devoted friend but, as this world goes, an honest man picked out of ten thousand, a character unique. No one like him ever crossed our path again.

That path itself was nearing a fork. After my wife and daughter had both gone and their ashes were buried among the great cedars on the margin of the swamp, the autumn parting from the wilderness became a solitary ritual.

The lake was usually calm then, its surface broken only by trout as they gulped drowned flying ants. The speedboats had disappeared, but an ancient man, clothed in toque and red mackinaw jacket, slowly rowed a punt of almost his own age to drag a spinner and baited hook. It was widely believed that he had caught a fish last spring.

Others like him, scornful of urban comforts, would spend the winter here. So would many of the birds, even some mallards and Canada geese. If the lake froze solid, they could escape to the seashore a few miles away. For several years, without fail, a big brown toad had visited our patio, unafraid of humans, and at closing time he seemed to regret our departure. But now he came no more. He had joined a numerous company of my friends.

On the way to the swamp I paused every year to glance up at the kids' abandoned and mouldering tree house, resolved every year to take it apart and never did. Where had its builders gone? Would some of them come back with their kids and rebuild the house? Would they clear the winter deadfall from the path, now carpeted with dry maple leaves, soft and springy underfoot? I hoped so.

The swamp still wore most of summer's garb, its ferns as high as my shoulder, its firs, cedars and hemlocks apparently untouched by the changing weather, its deciduous trees naked, the windless forest silent and, as I imagined, brooding on the season of gales ahead.

Then creak and growl would break the silence, trees would fall and snow flatten the underbrush. But for the time being, this massive organism of vegetables, animals, birds, insects and microscopic life emitted no whisper and seemed to rest, though its hidden labour did not pause for a single moment.

The swamp covered only an acre or so and had no special beauty except in the days of spring when trilliums, yellow violets and bleeding hearts bloomed at its soggy edge. And yet in all seasons it presented a glimpse of the ultimate mystery.

Unimaginable centuries ago, when the cosmic speck later called Earth was young and hot, life began in a swamp. There, vegetation took root, fish, animals and that improbable creature, *Homo sapiens,* kept evolving, with curious results.

Or so the men of science tell us, though they never explain the cause, purpose or meaning of evolution. Lacking any scientific knowledge, I left the swamp to manage its teeming life by its well-tried methods, above and below the ground.

For an interval not worth counting in this ageless laboratory, I had held its title deeds and it was not ravished in my time. Enough that the ashes buried there, mine included, would become a minute element in the grand process. Enough that I had seen, however briefly, a microcosm of all living things.

The swamp and its inhabitants were more interesting, I

judged, than all the famous spectacles of distant lands, the cities, arts and treasures of men. But I was prejudiced through age and memory. The stranger would see only some black, wet, oozing earth in a grove of mighty trees, centuries old though infants by the measurement of swamp time. With me, a minor plot of virgin forest summoned thoughts too deep for tears.

In the autumn of 1984—notable for more important reasons of state—camp closing disrupted our old habits. Everything went wrong at once.

When Dot and Joan had departed and my home was desolate, good luck arrived in the person of Gladys Veitch, a handsome widow no longer young but glowing with energy. She had been raised on a prairie farm, had trained as a nurse, practised her profession in many places, become an artist of cuisine and now began to manage all my domestic affairs, even driving me in her automobile wherever I wished to go.

On the eve of the national election, we were both sick in camp with flu, Gladys confined to her bed. I was still on my feet, though groggy. Since Gladys intended to support a certain political party (here nameless) and I would support its rival, our votes must cancel each other. I proposed, therefore, that we avoid a drive to town in dank, cold weather, since we could have no effect on the electoral outcome.

"Oh no, Mr. Hutchison," said Gladys. "If you don't vote you'll regret it till the end of your life. We have to vote."

Accordingly, it was resolved that, next day, we would visit the polling station near our Saanich house. In the meantime, as Gladys lay in bed and pain while I sat in the kitchen close to the stove, events moved rapidly.

Radar, the cat with deeply penetrating eyes, carried a rat into the bathtub, his favourite killing ground, and proceeded at leisure to demolish his prey. Nicky, our beloved mongrel dog, danced beside the tub, barking furiously. At that precise moment, a safety valve attached to the boiler sprang a leak, discharged a jet of scalding water and flooded the kitchen floor around me. Gladys moaned. The dog barked. The cat and the rat fought to the death. I opened the back door and vainly tried to sweep out the flood.

As the crisis deepened, my son appeared by chance to visit his cabin nearby. A skilled amateur plumber, he turned off the tap above the boiler and the deluge ceased. We cut a leather washer out of my belt and repaired the leaky valve.

Darkness had by now descended. The bathroom was silent at last, the tub smeared with the deceased rat's remains, the cat purring beside the stove, the dog asking for his supper, Gladys too ill, I assumed, to vote on the following day.

Unluckily, I had underestimated her patriotism. Next morning we braved a rainstorm, staggered along the muddy trail, drove to town, cancelled each other's vote and drove back to camp. There, Gladys returned to bed. Her conscience was clear and mine no longer troubled me. As citizens we had done our duty. But our influence had not seriously affected the nation's future. And we still had much work to do before the camp was sealed against winter.

In a few days the weather turned hot and dry, the year's last fire died in the stove, and the automobile was crammed with baggage, a mewing cat and a whining dog. I locked the cabin door, secreted the key where a blind burglar could find it and performed the final rite of emptying a bucket of water over the boxes of nasturtiums. They might live for several more weeks if rain came soon and frost late.

From the bend in the trail I looked back, as I had looked in farewell every year since my youth. The cabin, ugly in its tin sheath, would tremble in the winter tempests, sway under its burden of snow and, in my private fantasy, would hear again the voices that I had once heard. But abandoned, lonely, half forgotten, it would survive till spring though I might not come this way again.

At the Summit

DOT AND I were in our late fifties before we saw Canada in true perspective. We had travelled frequently across the nation by airplane, automobile and train, but not until we climbed a towering peak in the Rockies and, with our own wild surmise, looked down upon the endless distance and squared brown marquetry of the prairies did we begin to grasp the scope and splendour of the Canadian land. From our home the view, physical and mental, was narrow like the shelf beside the western sea. From the cold and naked spine of the continent, all Canada was visible to the imagination if not quite to the eye. At first by chance and then, year after year, by choice, we drove to the Rockies' eastern foothills in autumn's last golden days. We knew that winter, the real winter of a northern country, was not far off, and we sought the real frontier before snow closed it.

In our patch of coastal forest we could only pretend that we belonged to the wilderness. On the plains and mountains among folk unspoiled by urban progress, we might encounter authentic country life.

Outside Pincher Creek, Alberta, we found James Riviere. This archetypal mountain man, whom nobody called Jim, was tall and gaunt with a face of stretched leather. He was also taciturn and wary of strangers until he had tested us in the saddle and watched us in rough spots far beyond any trail. His lore was shared gradually and grudgingly, but at last we seemed to be accepted.

As a preliminary experiment, he took us on horseback up a gentle rise (or so he regarded it, though we panted for breath at such a height). Waiting patiently for us to recover, he communicated with his horses by telepathy (or so we suspected).

In camp James proved himself a skillful cook. Breakfast pancakes flavoured and dyed purple with huckleberries were his specialty, served in large numbers. We wasted none of them.

Next year, having judged that we could survive greater heights, he took us, three companions and a pair of wranglers, gaunt and leather-faced like him, into the heart of the Rockies. There we came upon some curious spectacles.

Hour by hour, sometimes minute by minute, the skyline advanced or retreated, changing its hue and texture, shimmering like silk or melting into blue liquid. The saddle and pack horses, long trained for this dangerous work, picked their way through dense jack pine thickets and over treacherous rock slides that diminished the mountains every year by an imperceptible fraction and will level them in a few million more centuries of erosion.

Meanwhile, we could observe their crenelated battlements and fretted spires, the lapidary mosaics of stone and lichen, the detritus of avalanche, the swath of dead trees, the caverns measureless to man. Beside our nightly campfire, we gazed at sidereal space. Against it, the mountains turned to silver, reef on reef, and the stars looked to be within reach of our hands. Relaxing after a hard day, Riviere informed us: "It's pretty up here, might pretty, I reckon."

Though he was cautious, his route of march often terrified us. On a huge roan mare, her neck bell tinkling to warn off grizzlies, he would lead our procession over shale slides that seemed to be impassable. Beyond them, some ledges were so narrow that we all dismounted, led our horses, kept our eyes away from the gulches and the inky ponds a thousand feet below us and gasped the thin air with bursting lungs.

Several days' ride from the nearest habitation, we must have been in danger of accidents, but none occurred, except for a horse rolling down a slope and twisting the leg of its woman rider. There were other risks. One day we awakened to find ourselves trapped by fog. The mountains were blotted out. Overhead, torn cloud fragments raced across the sky from west to east.

We were in the grip of a Pacific storm, Riviere said, and could not hope for immediate escape. With his sixth sense—his nose for weather—he sniffed the air and told me privately, "She's a bastard, all right, a proper bastard." After strolling down the valley, he returned to promise that the sun would shine before noon. And so it did.

When the fog lifted we scaled a steep hill of loose boulders to a ridge hardly ten feet wide above timber line. Suddenly the fog descended again. I could see Dot's steaming horse ahead of me but no farther. And then, just as suddenly, the wind veered and blew a hurricane from the east. The sun drilled through the clouds and set them whirling like giant snowflakes. Earth's solid stuff dissolved. The green of spruce, the gold of poplar and the blue of the valley tarns oozed together, changing and rechanging as in a kaleidoscope. I might have been a witness to Creation's first day.

Dot's horse reared, but she clung to her saddle. The pack horses bolted, scattering their baggage. James slid to the ground, held the bridle of his plunging mare and cursed. But in another minute the wind dropped, fog blinded us and the earth turned solid again.

After an hour's search the wranglers reassembled the pack train and gathered most of the baggage. In midafternoon Riviere led us through a mile of fallen and charred trees left by a forest fire. The wranglers had to cut some of them with axe and saw. Darkness and rain overtook us, but at last, soaked to the skin, we reached a level campsite.

Tents raised, a great fire burning, our clothes drying, our energies revived by Riviere's favourite remedy called moose milk, a mixture of hot water, sugar and whiskey, we ate and slept well. On the following day I was far from well. I shivered in hot sunlight and could eat nothing. A doctor in our company announced that a microbe had invaded me. He carried no medicine with him.

Riviere quickly dug up some wild strawberry plants and boiled the roots. Then he persuaded me to drink an unpleasant beverage. At breakfast next morning I demolished thirteen pancakes. Riviere had studied the Indians' pharmacopoeia and made good use of it. He chopped and ground turkey grass, a common weed, and spread a green pulp on our minor cuts and burns. They soon healed.

Having also studied the habits of animals, he brought us close to deer, elk and a conventicle of a dozen white-bearded goats as solemn as deacons at prayer, and a mother sheep who ran along the perpendicular wall of a high stone basin followed by her lamb, not yet half a year old.

We watched them with amazement, but Riviere was more interested in the soft ground where he had discovered big footprints.

"Grizzly," he said. "Must have been here a few minutes ago. Bell scared him off, I guess."

Since Riviere carried no gun, we were lucky that his mare wore her bell.

It was now getting late in the season. A wisp of snow had fallen on our last camp. Towards the end of the journey, a day's ride to his ranch, Riviere asked whether anyone cared to climb a pyramid on the margin of the foothills. The view from the top, he said, was worth seeing. But no horse would venture up this vertical scarp.

Dot alone volunteered, and I could not desert her. So Riviere guided the two of us up the mountain. After an hour's struggle we reached the peak. Here, in a foot of snow, we gazed down on the checkerboard prairie farms. The bounteous dimensions of our country and the human prodigy that had tamed it were spread before us to the horizon. We descended the pyramid with a new sense of perspective.

Fortunately, most of Canada was still untamed and, to the average Canadian, unknown. In our life together, Dot and I wandered into some unlikely places and learned to know their unlikely inhabitants. A portrait gallery of these men and women, the unmistakable outdoor breed, is vivid to me long after they have gone.

Especially vivid among them as winter comes again is Bill McGarrigle, a wiry little man of grooved face and dogged courage, a retired professional baseball pitcher who, destitute in the Great Depression, had carried buckets of rainbow trout minnows to stock lakes far above the North Thompson River valley. Since he could afford nothing better, he packed enough oatmeal to feed himself. By the time we rode into his region of thick forest, Bill and his wife, Arline, had built three cabins for mad fishermen like me. His fat rainbows snatched flies of any colour and were easily hooked but not easily landed. Bill prepared them for our winter use before our son and his friend could eat the whole smoked catch like candy.

When snow began to fall one morning, Bill ordered us out of camp right away. Tomorrow, he said, the trail might be blocked until spring. We rode all day through snowdrifts and swollen streams to reach the valley and our automobile in darkness. Now we found that the smoked trout had been left behind.

Our guide, next year, in the Clearwater region was a very different sort of man from McGarrigle—tall, strong, blond, square of face and reluctant in speech. Ted Helset had come from Norway, built a house and barn at the end of a rough, crooked road, trapped fur animals in winter, survived a forest fire by inches, killed an attacking grizzly with his last bullet at a distance of three feet, broken a leg when he was alone in the bush and, starving, was found after a week.

When Dot, our son and I drove to Helset's little ranch, he was still limping after a year in the Kamloops hospital. But he agreed to take us up the Clearwater and, on his white horse, rode at a fast pace. We followed as best we could through heavy timber and at nightfall reached a comfortable log house with a corral around it.

At dawn next morning we started out for a lake where Helset had planted trout fry years earlier. Arriving at this secret sanctuary by noon, we found that the rainbows weighed five pounds or more. Ignorant of human predators, they would eagerly swallow our flies, wet and dry, until we tired of catching them and belatedly realized that dusk was falling.

Helset led us back to camp in darkness, across deep, foaming streams, boulders and muskeg. We were frightened as he rode at a gallop, but this evidently was his normal speed. Lying bravely, we assured him that we had enjoyed the ride.

On a later expedition, we reconnoitered the Ashnola valley long before a road or even a trail had been built there from Keremeos. Our guide, whose name escapes me, was a man of sturdy frame, jolly disposition and well-educated speech. Along the way he showed us an ancient trick of the Indians.

Sighting half a dozen fool grouse hens on a small tree, he dismounted, took a lace from his boot, fastened a loop to the end of a long stick and, one by one, jerked the stupid birds to the ground. His operation was quite legal in the open grouse season.

We feasted that night and, on the morrow, climbing on foot to a rocky pinnacle, glimpsed the faint blue line of the Coast Range. As clearly to us as from Riviere's pyramid, looking eastward, the country's dimensions were again visible looking westward.

Though I well remember the name and looks of another guide, they cannot be disclosed here. Beside the campfire one night, this squat, hairy man, an immigrant from central Europe, explained his lucrative winter trapping methods and added: "Us trappers, we meet and talk about income tax. But we won't pay it on account of we figger it's no good."

Nor did he pay the excise tax on liquor. Instead, he manufactured his own alcohol by a technique learned in his homeland. Since the process required oak sawdust to strain poisonous elements out of the distilled liquid, he collected discarded oak furniture in the nearest villages and sawed it at leisure. The resulting potation, he said, was excellent both for drinking and for cauterizing wounds. He never travelled without it, but gladly accepted my offer of legal rye from a government store.

Our guides were frontiersmen, usually on the move, gambling their lives in daily peril, not country men or cultivators settled on the land. But atop Pavilion Mountain, we had long known the land's harsh mandate.

Ernest Carson's ranch, established by his father in the days of the Cariboo gold rush, was a saucer of fields and open range high above the Fraser River's winding ribbon, and yet it was surrounded by mountains still higher.

In all seasons we found warm welcome in the original ranch house that Ernest had rebuilt. If he was busy on the ranch, we rode with his comely wife, Halcyon (who later manhandled a pair of stiff-necked eminent British Columbians), out to the rim of the Fraser's abyss or the bluff overlooking the necklace of the three Marble Canyon lakes, each a different gem of blue or green, depending on the day's sunlight.

In summer nights we breathed the perfume of clover and alfalfa, heard the chuckle of the irrigation ditches and the eerie laugh of the coyotes. In winter we helped to shovel snow around the house and barns or rode toboggans down a nearby hill.

Ernest's life as a landsman was disciplined and hard. He had fought in the first war and afterwards was accounted the best horseman in the Cariboo and, better, a natural spokesman in the provincial legislature for the ranching community. But even when he became minister of public works and built many of British Columbia's modern highways, I think he regretted leaving his years of country life on Pavilion. And when he dropped dead in his Victoria garden, a happy chapter in our lives had ended.

In middle age, Dot and I had driven from Halifax to Victoria with many detours, a total distance of some twenty thousand miles, and we had seen much of Canada's fair estate. Since then it has produced one of the world's most urbanized societies, a small minority of its people living a country life outside the cities and big towns. In my old age, I decided to take a final look at the land itself and, if possible, to renew my friendship with survivors of earlier days.

With Gladys Veitch driving her new automobile and efficiently managing all the arrangements, we crossed British

Columbia and the prairies by a meandering route. Though it was very late in autumn, the weather remained sunny. We hoped that winter's arrival would be late, too.

A graduate of farm life, Mrs. Veitch knew the history and thoughtways of her native heath. To me the prairies were a montage of tawny stubble fields, shattering crimson dawns and sunsets, huge, round hay bales, broad-shouldered grain elevators, beef cattle numberless, mile-long freight trains like children's toys on the far horizon, geese in myriads flying southward and filling the sky with their hoarse cry and the rustle of their wings.

For the people of the west coast, or those of Ontario, Quebec and the Maritimes, the swath of flat land between the Great Lakes and the Rockies is a report in the newspapers, an economic problem, a contest of mysterious local politics, almost a foreign state. The central plains become a reality when you see them at first hand, stop in their little towns and talk to their people. Since I had last travelled here much had changed, generally for the better. The cities and towns had doubled or tripled in population, built skyscrapers and snug new homes, surrounding them with gardens, transforming the whole prairie landscape.

But the land had not changed, and as in pioneer times farming was still a gamble of rain, drought and food prices. Only a strong and peculiar breed of men and women could plant and harvest the crop. Nowadays they needed at least a square mile of good land, preferably two sections, with about half a million dollars worth of machinery. But like the land, the instincts of its occupants hadn't changed, either, and even the farmers who move to town can never discard their heritage.

An old cattleman like Bert Sheppard of High River, Alberta, that well-groomed snug town of famous legendry on the Whoop-up Trail, has become a legend himself. He often travels the world and could live anywhere, but he returns to his original bailiwick as surely as one of his horses to its home range.

In his late eighties Bert, once a professional broncobuster, likes to ride a quiet mount and survey the rolling foothills, behind them the blue and white marching line of the Rockies. No man accustomed to such a spectacle is likely to desert it. From here the political controversies of Ottawa, the financial triumphs or disasters of Toronto and the search for a Canadian identity established long ago, mainly by the land and its stern decrees, seem insignificant and unreal.

As we drove homeward I asked myself a nagging question, seldom asked in Parliament or press. Can a handful of people, failing to reproduce their numbers in a crowded world, permanently hold a land of transcontinental expanse, of riches, freedom and grandeur? That question would not be answered in my time nor in my grandchildren's. But no matter how Canadians managed their estate, the land would remain, always the land and the impulses nourished by it from the beginning.

Halfway through the Rockies real winter overtook us, but its cold and fury did not depress us, for we had beheld a broad segment of real country life.

The Year's
Low Tide

AT ITS BEGINNING, the night of dreadful memory in our young days outside Victoria was calm. A gentle breeze ruffled the slim lombardy poplars beside the road. Clouds like fleece moved slowly across the crescent of a new moon. Except for an owl's croak the December countryside was mute.

But just before dawn we were roused from sleep by an explosion of sound, then the creak of rending wood and a sequence of hollow drumbeats. Leaping from bed, I could hardly stand on the balcony against the wind, but in the half-light I saw the poplars bent almost double and a big gap in the oak spinney. The lawn had disappeared under a tangled mass of branches.

As full daylight came, the wind died, and now we found our front door blocked, the huge trunk of our oldest oak lying on the driveway. In its fall it had carried with it a fine dogwood. Our daughter's automobile was squashed flat. Another oak, broken near the ground, hung and swayed above the corner of the house. None of the supple poplars but five oaks, all more than a yard in diameter and two centuries in age, had fallen that night.

A crew of hired woodsmen needed a week to chainsaw the trunks and pile up some ten cords of fuel. Dot and I dragged the smaller branches to the field for burning and exhausted ourselves close to the point of collapse.

Apparently the weather was demented. Two days after the gale we could see no farther than a dozen feet through the fog. I groped my way down the lane with the sense of walking on water. This scene, I imagined, must be like the ancient Greeks' idea of the dismal region beyond the Styx. But presently the sun burned off the mist curtain and in the evening sank through a sky of flame.

While inland Canadians, long hardened to ice and blizzard, envy our genial climate and believe that it spoils us, few of them have seen its cranky moods. Few Victorians, indeed, can remember the historic winter of 1916, when the city was paralyzed overnight, the school closed, the youngsters enraptured by three feet of snow. Disaster on that scale did not occur again, but we seldom escaped snowfall of minor, manageable depth. Not long after our mighty oaks fell, we were shovelling a narrow path from the house to the lane and brushing snow off our shrubs before it could break them.

Its quality was much inferior to the continental variety—so adhesive, so filled with moisture and so heavy that, shovelling it, we risked cardiac arrest. On the other hand, it soon melted and then, in a week of frost, ponderous icicles hung from branches above our reach and tore them from the trunks.

Snow might fall even before Christmas, and once the thermometer registered zero Fahrenheit in October. Four of our apple trees were killed. At the December solstice, when the planet began to turn its northern flank southward, I wondered, absurdly, how long its inhabitants could rely on this convenient routine, which, after all, had sometimes changed in the past, with spectacular results. But lengthening daylight by mid-January reassured me.

In our young days we welcomed the occasional visits of Canadian winter. They made us appreciate our unearned coastal privileges.

Between the plum trees of the Rogers orchard—a challenging hazard—we rode sleighs downhill, our young children on our

backs, and we skated over the frozen swamp at the bottom of
the lane. The countryside, dressed in white, looked as beautiful
as the rest of Canada, the sun radiant, every twig bejewelled,
tree shadows cleanly printed on the snow.

But our enjoyment of the national climate was always brief.
Unlike the inlanders, we preferred the mild, damp, misty atmosphere of the seacoast. Then, at night, we heard the fog horns of
Juan de Fuca Strait groaning like wounded marine animals on
the graveyard of the Pacific where many good ships had
perished. What vessels were now struggling through the narrow gateway to the continent? Some of them, even with radar
equipment, were likely to shatter against the Island rocks.

Our fogs, said Rawling, could not be compared to the real
peasoupers of his native London, but "they're good enough,"
he added, with giggles and dimples, "for a poor little colony
like Canada." Anyhow, they were thick enough for us.

When the sun failed to disperse them, the air was soon
cleansed by the rain that distant Canadians always exaggerate in
their odd notion of the coast, as if its climate were uniform. In
fact most of the ocean clouds stream across the low hills of Vancouver Island's southern tip, collide with the mainland mountains and unload their cargo on the Vancouver metropolis. Victoria's rainfall is less than that of many eastern cities, and its
summer drought is often prolonged. But on the western shore
of the Island, the precipitation is sometimes the heaviest in
Canada.

Snape was not impressed. "Rain?" he said. "Chrissake, you
'aven't seen rain till you've seen the monsoon in Injia. The
ground's baked solid one day, and next day I've swam across it
and bloody lucky to come out alive. Snow? You've seen no
snow like in those bloody 'Imalayas. A man's blood gets thin
'ere, orful thin. We're run down an' worn to a frazzle."

I did not question the word of a veteran British soldier. Perhaps Snape was right. Climate, I sometimes thought, had
depraved us, corrupted our ancestral Canadian virtue. Usually it
was put to harsh test at the Christmas season, when the Pacific
hurled the year's worst storms upon the Island to break seawalls
and power lines.

About that time, we would be defying the weather and, drip-
ping wet, chilled to the bone, would cut holly from the hedge
planted at the start of our country life and, since then, neglected.
Year after year, Dot and I chose the stalks with the most berries,
packed and mailed them to our prairie and eastern friends. With
us, holly was easily grown and commonplace, but it delighted
them as a token of cheer, a promise of spring from a land of
sirens and lotus eaters where we supposedly lived in sunshine
and eternal afternoon.

According to unbreakable custom I spent part of Christmas
Day pruning fruit trees—a grave responsibility—because a
young tree, once mistreated, could never be reshaped. Why, in
my old age, I continued to prune trees nearly as old, when all
their summer's fruit would be stolen, I don't know. But a tradi-
tion of more than six decades could not be lightly disregarded.

As long as kids frolic and chatter in the house, Christmas is a
jolly festival. After they grow up, separate and have families of
their own, the time of holiday loses its magic. Besides, the mass
of Christ has been defamed and vulgarized as a strictly commercial proposition all over the Western world; a hired Santa
Claus in every department store, at its entrance a Salvation
Army lass ringing a bell and collecting money for the poor—
this to hallow the birth of a Child who possessed nothing by
today's reckoning.

Instead of observing a Christian rite in the modest style of our
grandparents, we joined in a midwinter revel familiar to pagan
societies throughout the ages. Doubtless it was the best we
could do in a worldwide culture dedicated to the worship of the
great god Gross National Product. Anyhow, the revel did no
damage except to some old-fashioned Christians, their numbers
small. It helped many unfortunates through their barren cele-
bration and brought out, for a week or two, the decent qualities
of the fortunate.

Still, it was a meagre substitute for the Christmas of my
boyhood, when I first beheld a living, laughing, jingling Santa
Claus in some Prescott church hall and didn't recognize a
woman dressed up in crimson, stuffed with a pillow and disguised with a beard of cotton batting.

My numerous aunts, devout Christians and unfailing atten-
dants at their church, bought toys for me in Ogdensburg, New
York, and smuggled them, under expansive skirts, across the
St. Lawrence ice. But they always supported the Conservative
Party's high tariffs to restrict imports of American goods.

Christmas in the little town of British Columbia also supplied
plenty of toys, which I wound up and quickly demolished.
Among the town characters, none is clearer in memory than old
Tex, custodian of the livery stable, his sagging jowls,
moustache stained yellow by tobacco, red-rimmed eyes and
whiskey breath. He gave me a genuine fifty-cent piece. Though
rarely sober, he had the true Christian spirit.

Alas, by the time I reached Victoria my faith in Santa had
been expunged, but I instilled it in my own children, who lost it
at the normal age and instilled it in theirs.

Having become an octogenarian just before Mrs. Veitch took
charge of my house, I found her, at Christmas, to be a Dick-
ensian character straight out of Dingley Dell. She garnished a
shapely fir tree cut in our woods, filled stockings with charming
little gifts, hung them by the fireplace and cooked a turkey dinner that Lucullus would envy. Through the window we could
see the tiny yellow stars glistening on the jasmine bush to serve
as a humble reminder of the first Christmas and some wondering shepherds in a far country long ago.

After the holidays, medical scientists inform us, Canadians
are inflicted by the "blahs," a sudden inertia peculiar to the inhabitants of a northern climate. This native disorder saps the
vigour of the body and dulls the mind, while accentuating Canada's frigid identity unrecognizable at warmer seasons.

In my travels I formed the opposite impression of a race phys-
ically invigorated, mentally stimulated and inwardly warmed
by the cold. No blahs were visible among outdoor workers
drilling oil wells, cutting timber, building skyscrapers or feeding cattle. In the towns the clubs, societies and organizations of
all sorts were bustling, the local machines of politics and business revolving at maximum speed, youngsters learning hockey
on flooded school grounds, old folk curling, everybody active
at work or play and talking by telephone more than any other

people in the world. The myth of a stern and silent northern people dies hard.

If the cold does slow down some inland Canadians, they have good reason for their blahs, but we have none on the coastland. We can work in our gardens or play golf through most winters, and yet as the years passed I was increasingly depressed by grey skies and drizzle. My spirits faltered in the mist, and I shivered in temperatures that, away from the coast, would be considered springlike.

More and more I huddled indoors watching the seagulls glide westward at daybreak and eastward at dusk to their safe roosts on the islands of Georgia Strait. When my bravado in the summer woods had leached out, the vitality of those birds rebuked my idleness. So did the men who drove the neighbourhood trucks, fed the milk cows, built houses or, among the privileged classes, followed little white balls around the golf links.

It was no comfort to hear professors of great universities argue that we live in a decadent epoch closely resembling the last days of the Roman Empire. In my ignorance of history, the parallel of overburdening armaments, strangling bureaucracy, crime, bread and political circuses seemed only too accurate.

But the countryside and the wilderness remained. And just as I began to doubt the eternal verities, the daylight visibly increased and the first seed catalogues, those old tempters, arrived in my postbox. The planet had successfully rounded its solstitial curve again. Now a mysterious chemistry rekindled even my feeble energies, and none too soon. For in midwinter our lonely camp was in need of them.

Song of
the Fire

ON HEARING of Thomas Hardy's death, Christopher Morley, the famous American writer, lighted a bonfire in the yard of his Long Island home because, he said, "fire is element." It fittingly celebrated the primal power of Hardy's books.

I was slow to understand Morley and his fable even when I met and talked with him at length. But after he had gone, I saw in fire some elements that he, and Hardy also, had missed without a virgin forest to supply them.

In January, the month of the two-faced god who looks backward to the old year and forward to the new, we burned last summer's accumulation of brush at the camp. This was no easy task when the mountainous pile had been soaked by weeks of rain. But with plenty of dry newspapers stored in the cabin—their important news mostly reversed by events—dry kindling from the woodshed and a worn-out automobile tire, we had the makings of a blaze.

Though the use of rubber introduced artificial elements into the wilderness and seemed an unsporting and unworthy device, it got the fire off to a fast start. Besides, we were too old now to quibble over any help we could summon.

Dr. Samuel Johnson, no outdoor man, apparently had learned, at second-hand no doubt, something about combustion and told his faithful Bozzy that "knowledge always desires increase; it is like fire which must first be kindled by some external agent but which will afterwards propagate itself."

This was true as far as it went. Even in the worst weather our fires quickly propagated themselves and swallowed a foot of snow with a single hissing gulp. But as Johnson, addict of the London streets, could not know, a fire in the wilderness is much more than a chemical reaction of oxygen and carbon, a mixture of elements in Morley's fable.

To us it was the audible record of the days since spring. For the ear sensitive enough to distinguish its many voices, fire echoes, in minor key, the crackle of the summer path, the buzz of insects, the song of birds, the rumble of storm, the crash of falling trees. On its funeral pyre the forest seems to utter the memories of its lifetime.

Old Omar, inhabitant of the desert, might burn his winter garments of repentance, but to Canadians fire tells a different story. They have used it, often prodigally, to clear the farmland of half a continent, burning and plowing their way from coast to coast. And even we clumsy arsonists could translate the message of the flames. They leaped, forked and spoke in separate tongues, broke into scarlet splinters and danced merrily over the debris of the year. We watched, we listened and we breathed deep the immemorial incense of wood smoke.

In summer, throughout the day and much of the night, human and mechanical sounds disturbed the forest. In winter we had it alone to ourselves and might have been a hundred miles from civilization. On a windless day only the voices of the fire broke the silence. The sparks flew straight up in harmless myriads. At times the heat drove us away until the flames subsided into a cone of glowing embers and a circle of black sticks. These we raked to the centre, and the flames and sparks mounted again.

To lug countless sodden, heavy branches even for a distance of twenty feet and lay them, parallel, on the fire, demanded more energy in one day than the summer's work of lugging them out of the woods. But now we had the support of Archie, the white-bearded, red-nosed local sage. At the first rise of smoke from our camp he would paddle down the lake in his canoe and volunteer his physical labour and expert advice. When the flames were a dozen feet high he noted that our method of ignition was wrong and shameful.

"To think," he said, "you needed a tire, a dude's easy way, a waste of good rubber, a crime. All you needed was a knife to cut some shavings. But no, you were too lazy, too soft. Ha, when I was prospectin' for gold in the mountains of Mexico and run out of matches, that didn't stop me. I lighted my fires with the old Indian trick. I rubbed two pieces of dry wood together."

Since Archie and I agreed that our conversations would not be restricted by anything as dull as the truth, his Mexican adventures, like his participation in the Cariboo gold rush more than a century earlier, were unquestioned.

Having recounted these and other exciting tales, he would recline on a smooth, mossy rock, well dried by the fire, and light his pipe with several matches while Dot and I continued to lug branches.

I had long admired his mastery of the pipe. It gave him an air of subliminal wisdom, a mature and commanding look. A man who could smoke in this lordly fashion, I thought, could do anything when, poisoned with nicotine and still healthy, he could endure anything. Repeated trials and failures convinced me that I would never be a successful pipe smoker. But I didn't cease to try until I was as old as Archie. Then I gave up tobacco in humiliation and despair.

Comfortable on the rock, Archie observed that it had been smoothed by the glaciers of the last ice age and in due time they would again cover the land around us. Accordingly, Canada's life must be short. However, the glacial threat was less alarming than the prospect of another spring.

"You can smell it already," he said, though our nostrils registered only smoke. "It's on the way and it'll bring the dudes from town, packs of 'em, as sure as death and taxes and worse than both, and life won't be worth livin' any more. Oh God, how I dread the spring, the cocktail crowd, the speedboats, all hell breakin' loose. It's enough to drive a man to drink."

When we paused for sandwiches in the cabin and produced a

bottle of distilled warmth from its hiding place, Archie cheered up remarkably. After a couple of stiff drinks beside the stove, he regaled us with the gossip of the village, the wide-ranging amours of Bill McGillicuddy, who cooked hamburgers at a joint in Duncan and would have to marry, perhaps bigamously, his latest girl friend before (as Archie explained with delicacy) a certain event occurred.

As for himself, he had not married because his father, grand-father and all his male ancestors through generations in-numerable were bachelors. To that good old family custom a man of honour naturally conformed.

After more drinks he even distinguished us from the horror of urban company. On his second thoughts it appeared that, de-spite our imperfections, we were unlike the general run of dudes, so unlike indeed that if a deep snowfall should endanger our cabin's roof he promised to shovel it off, if the trail re-mained passable as it certainly would not.

He watched us work all afternoon, not lifting a single branch. Again deploring our combustion methods, he paddled home, taking with him the bottle and its remaining contents. Still, he had earned his modest reward. Next week, lacking better mate-rial, I put the facts of his kindly assistance into printed fiction.

Our winter visits were usually less pleasant. We often found a spot of blood or a little clump of feathers on the snow where a rabbit, a mouse or a bird had met some predator. Once we saw the footprints of a cougar, and its claw marks were distinct on the bole of a maple tree. Evidently its hunt for deer had failed. No bones lay hereabouts. In one winter of heavy snow, a deer sought refuge under a neighbour's sun porch and starved to death.

Twice, willow grouse flew through the cabin windows. The first of them died instantly. The second remained alive. Unable to escape its prison, it survived miraculously for thirteen days without food or water until we happened to visit the camp and found it half dead on the floor among shards of glass. We laid it on the patio beside a bowl of water and a scattering of oatmeal, sure that it could not recover, and left it there. When we came back ten minutes later that extraordinary bird had flown away.

The story of the late Oscar Bass, a prominent Victoria law-
yer, unfolded on a far larger, nobler scale.

Bass had once owned a mile of lake shoreline, had sold most
of it but kept extensive acreage on the hill across the road. At his
house in town he awaited the milk wagon every morning and
fed a lump of sugar to a piebald horse, Buster by name.

Eventually the milkman announced that a truck must soon replace Buster, who would be transformed into canned meat for
dogs and cats. This news appalled Bass, then deputy attorney
general of British Columbia and a respected public figure. Although he was close to seventy years old, he instantly bought
the horse—even older in animal chronology—and had it carried
by truck to his country place.

There, in spite of his age and height of about five feet, he built
a shed and cleared by hand a fenced yard for Buster's retirement.
Summer or winter, the lucky horse fattened on bales of hay and
sacks of oats brought from Victoria at his owner's expense.
Each weekend, in all seasons, Bass visited Buster to make sure
he was comfortable.

Buster lived a life of leisure and luxury for some four years.
Then Bass discovered the horse's body, the neck broken by a
fall over a ditch. Grieving as for a human friend, Bass dug a
grave for Buster and buried him. Only a few survivors of those
days remember the man, the horse or the grave.

Even less remembered is the benevolence of the late Dr.
Charlie Duck, a veteran anaesthetist in Victoria's main hospital.
He owned a place beside the lake some miles from us, and he
loved the animal residents nearby. His affection for a band of
raccoons was so steadfast that, once a week or more often in
cold winters, he drove up from town with supplies of bread,
biscuits and meat. Tramping through the snow, he fed his
pensioners and their young. They were greedy, but he loved
them.

The weather, unfortunately, was not as steadfast as men like
Bass and Duck. In January we never knew what might greet us
in the woods. On every winter visit they seemed different.

When snow has fallen, the alder and maple leaves, the sword
ferns, bracken and wildflower stalks lay crushed flat. After a

rainy spell, the ground oozed and squished underfoot, rivulets flowed into the black pool of the swamp, and we heard the gurgle of moving water as if it bubbled and boiled in a pot, stone cold. On a day of storm, Coleridge's Ancient Mariner, gripped by the Antarctic ice, could accurately describe this forest. High above us, the wind and the battered tree tops cracked and growled and roared and howled like noises in a swound. When the gale quickened we could almost hear from the enchanted kingdom of Kubla Khan a woman wailing for her demon lover. And yet, near the ground, the air was motionless. A spider's web, hung on a bush last autumn, still carried its tiny load of glistening dew.

Always there were some fallen trees. Since no ears had caught the thud of their fall, had it really made any sound? On the old enigma dividing philosophers and scientists we did not long brood. Nor did we stay long in the forest that hated and repelled all invaders. From its dark cavern and lurking ghosts, we retreated to the clear margin of the lake.

Here, the sky was dappled by clouds of a kind scarce in other seasons—fat, pink-edged and turning to pale green and violet at their rims. Or the long streaks of mares' tails foretold more storms.

Would the cabin survive them? Would the overhanging trees fall on the frail roof? There was no insurance against such risks, but we did what we could to protect our summer hide-out. Blown aside in places, the tin sheath must be screwed tight to the verandah posts, blocked gutters cleared of pine needles, perhaps a small leak repaired and occasionally the nests of mice or squirrels removed from a cozy mattress.

Then, until spring, we left the cabin and the forest to the weather, to the solitude and to our memories.

A Time
of Folly

ABOUT THE MIDDLE OF FEBRUARY, in my latter years, I always resolved not to plant another vegetable garden. That was a sane decision when I lacked the energy needed for digging, weeding, hoeing, thinning and spraying. At the same time, I was seized by a notion clearly insane—a dread of the approaching spring, a yearning for the next winter. Archie feared the dudes' invasion, I feared the workload in the days ahead. To minimize it, no vegetables would be planted.

My resolution lasted perhaps a week and collapsed with the arrival of the seed catalogues, those old seducers that brandished gorgeous pictures of edible crops never seen in this world. Year after year I put the catalogues aside for immediate burning, their temptation boldly rejected. But year after year I hesitated, and the hesitation was fatal. The seeds were ordered and digging began.

Jimmy, my gardening helper and faithful friend, was a fast digger and seemed to enjoy his mastery of the shovel. Watching him, I suspected that his smooth, unconsciously graceful motions harmonized with the portable radio hanging on a nearby post and emitting varied music to satisfy all tastes. Or if political speeches interrupted the music, Jimmy listened to them also, but he would not reveal how he voted at election time.

"That's personal and secretious," he once warned me, his grooved face set in hard lines, and I never asked again.

Concerning his work he was less discreet. As he enriched the soil with nature's fertilizer from the stable across the lane, the inventor of a new English vocabulary paused to observe that the farmer's latest gift was "coloshious" and "the best damn stuff goin' around here or they're not makin' it no more." He had no grounds for anxiety. The herd of fat Holstein dairy cows was making plenty of it, and their generous owner freely shared his wealth.

I left Jimmy digging and listening to the radio while I inspected the latest portents of spring.

The first crocuses of fragile look, pale-blue colour and golden pistil had appeared in the meadow where they had seeded them-selves and now opened under sunshine and closed like vertical umbrellas under passing clouds. Honeybees from a neighbour's hive buzzed impatiently as they extracted the crocus nectar.

Snowdrops had bloomed at Christmas, spreading beyond the flower beds into the oak woods and even breaking through cracks in the black-topped path. Each bloom carried three white petals and a second tier with green spots, perfectly heart-shaped, as if these brave little heralds of spring knew the date of February 14 and offered us a valentine.

That such exquisite patterns and colours resulted from blind accident or random evolution seemed to me the wildest of all fancies in this scientific age. But my reflections, like Jimmy's political views, were personal and undiscussed with more practical-minded friends. I, too, could be secretious.

The expert digger kept digging, the radio kept blaring, I rescued the surviving leeks from last year's garden, Mrs. Veitch converted them into ambrosial soup of her own unique formula and, inexorably, the season advanced.

Little time was left for winter's final job. I still had many orchard trees to prune and some, dead or dying, to cut. Those planted sixty years ago no longer bore much fruit, but, replacing them with dwarf trees for easier attention, I felt like the executioner of old servants. I also felt my own age as I clipped, chopped and sawed and dragged branches to the burning pile. This was slow drudgery. A single tree might keep me on a swaying ladder most of the afternoon, and yet the commercial growers of Okanagan and Niagara pruned their trees by the hundreds. I envied their strength and the equality of their fruit.

By now we had more firewood—oak, apple, plum, pear and cherry—than we could ever use. Though a notorious miser of fuel at the camp, I began to give some of it away in town. Living beside one of the world's great forests, the townspeople regarded an evening fire as too expensive and seldom allowed themselves that luxury. With us it cost only my labour.

In a winter of otherwise monotonous jobs, I summoned up enough will power to take apart for the bonfire the crumbling structure of boards and shingles that had once been the playhouse of a happy, boisterous little girl, whom I would not see again.

Later in that February, I came upon a mystery. As my six-foot handsaw gradually penetrated the three-foot trunk of a fallen oak, I heard the unmistakable rasp of metal grating against metal. Impossible, I thought. There could be no metal near the core of a tree more than a century old. Doubting my ears, I withdrew the saw and noticed that several of its teeth were blunted. With a sharp axe, I chopped around the original cut and found that a nail had been driven into the oak when it was barely six inches thick.

A blacksmith must have made the flat, square-headed nail in the early times of Governor James Douglas and his Fort Victoria. But who drove that iron splinter? Nobody will ever know. The oak had enfolded it under a new layer of wood each year and locked the secret in its heart.

Why, by one chance among a thousand, did my saw happen to touch the spot where the splinter lay? Was my discovery the result of blind luck or deliberate purpose? Had some man long ago left a message, sure that I would receive it?

Of course my whimsy was absurd, like others in my private hoard. But I saved the nail and pretended that it was driven to tell the finder about the work of skilled and daring men who had roamed this land before his time.

All humans store rusted nails of memory in their hearts, undisclosed to anyone and buried with them. Ours is the age of open communication, not of secrecy, or so goes the current myth. Politicians, evangelists, advertisers and trained communicators drive their nails of ambition and greed into the world's mind, day and night. If, at some remote time, our mores are surgically examined, like my oak, the autopsy will expose a vast store of worthless metal. By print or electric currents, information pours out to brainwash us until our brain cells become toughened against the intruders.

Yet somewhere, right now, a man or woman unknown is fashioning a new nail of truth or, more likely, repolishing an old and better one for discovery when it is needed to hold the battered house of society together. And so, as a pitiable gesture of faith in mankind, I drove the Fort Victoria blacksmith's nail into a young living oak. Perhaps a saw or axe will touch it after all my companions and I have been forgotten.

When Dot was still with me, we found, besides the nail, three different relics of early times. These chipped stone arrowheads had fallen on the meadow now temporarily belonging to us. But in historical reckoning, the Indians who had shot the arrows were recent arrivals, Johnnies-come-lately, from Asia. Earlier immigrants had preceeded them by several millennia. The nail in our oak had been driven only yesterday, perhaps to hang the carcass of a deer killed by an arrow.

Jimmy was indifferent to such local history and resented observers as he solemnized his annual rite, a massive fire of prunings from the orchard and shrubberies. He wanted to be alone in this job and may have communed with the many voices of the flames as we did at the camp, though how he heard them above the blare of his radio we could not guess.

All he would say at the morning coffeebreak was that the fire had gone ahead pretty good and the nation backward pretty fast. While his economic views lacked detailed facts, he had the advantage of a natural wisdom peculiar to men of his sort. Two years in advance he had predicted the business slump of 1981, because "things got all crazy and disluted." By the autumn of 1987, he repeated that warning just before the stock market crashed.

Jimmy's hunches didn't surprise me. The common folk on our lane or in town, I had found, were often wiser, by instinct, than governments and economists with their profound research and computerized figures.

"Those guys," said Jimmy, "had ought to be commuted and excarified. It's frustulating."

The lexicographer grinned and, finishing his muffins, thanked Mrs. Veitch for "your glorious endeavourments."

Until the spring rush, I had ample time to read and speculate on many provocative and incongruous notions. Books, I had learned, were one of the few comforts left to age and solitude. With some old men like me, books became an addiction, a vice incorrigible.

If the addicts cannot be reformed, they can defy all conventions and the overeducated literary snobs who inflict their own reading habits on those weak enough to listen. I was weak but not that weak. Too old for education or any mental improvement, I was free at last to read what I pleased, all the way between Shakespeare and detective stories or spy thrillers.

Certainly an honest book addict should frequently reread *Hamlet, The Pickwick Papers* and Sherlock Holmes, but I have known decent men who refused to do it. Percy Rawling's addiction, for example, was a worship of Dickens almost religious, and though he read voraciously while collecting numberless books, he had abandoned Shakespeare. "Not my man," he said, as if that explained his impiety. "But you might like him."

I liked him at irregular intervals. Regrettably preferring a few pages of Boswell at bedtime every night, I stumbled on Dr. Johnson's pronouncement that Shakespeare had never published more than seven lines without a flaw in them. Percy had gone before I could tell him of this gratifying discovery.

We agreed on the virtues of Chesterton, whose tattered book

of youthful essays I read annually at camp and found reassurance in his professional view that it was easier to write a dozen leading editorials for *The Times* of London on the salvation of the world than to invent a single joke on the follies of mankind.

At my own lowly grade of journalism I had reached the same conclusion, often sinking still lower to save the world in unread commentary. Not often could I rise, with heavy labour, to the lofty stratum of a light piece about nature and the countryside that happily might seem to have been dashed off in a moment of absentmindedness.

Jack Wilson, the chief justice, was the best read among my friends. He never travelled without a book containing all Shakespeare's plays, and he could recite many of their lines by heart. But he bitterly denounced critics and dilettantes who pretended to find therein meanings, symbols and arcane allusions unsuspected by the playwright.

When shelves in every room of our house were crammed with books, I often wondered what must happen to them after my departure. Probably they would go to a secondhand store, my close-knit, printed family broken up, the waifs and orphans separated, most of them doubtless ending, unread and forgotten, in some distant attic or garbage dump.

Meanwhile, book thieves never cease nor repent their crimes. Men and women, respectable in all other habits, borrow books of priceless value to the owner and fail to return them. Charles Lamb, evidently an unscrupulous borrower, might plead with tortured logic that books belonged to those who most appreciated them, but he was the immortal Elia and possibly could be forgiven. The ordinary thief (often a man's close friend) can offer no excuse. In a just society he would suffer condign, or capital punishment.

A lighter penalty would be applied to the specious reader who, like a water bug, skims the surface of a book, memorizes some brief paragraphs and talks learnedly of the author's message. But those offenders should not go scot free. What use is our Charter of Rights and Freedoms if it cannot defend the poor man's treasures?

While books are the most faithful companions of age and the

surest anodyne for its ills, nobody, however addicted, gets through many volumes in a lifetime, but all addicts exaggerate their literary travels. A simple calculation shows that a man who reads two serious books a week for half a century will digest only 5200, and few of us achieve this figure when new books surge from the world's presses in ceaseless flood to drown the strongest swimmer.

These facts should be ignored as too discouraging. The staunch and dogged reader, a natural pack rat always increasing his cache, does well to flounder through half of it. Like a doomed Sisyphus, he struggles against time and the gods in hopeless contest. Always he fails. If they are printed on good paper, books will outlast him by centuries.

Even more companionable in the dark, lonely months, but, alas, of shorter life, are dogs.

My experience with dogs began when I was four years old in a little British Columbia village near a native Indian reserve. Barnabas, one of the Indians, used a string to measure my feet, and his wife sewed buckskin moccasins to fit them. Barnabas also brought me a spotted mongrel pup, Nitchie by name. It soon died and was followed by a rough-haired fox terrier, who swam for fun across the west arm of Kootenay Lake; then Bodah, a Scottish terrier, who lived sixteen years; and later, in our country place, a succession of dogs, some of them sickly, one violently insane, another dedicated to the extermination of the farmer's chickens, and yet another who wounded and would have killed a fawn in our woods if I hadn't arrived just in time to save it.

This record, on the whole, seemed depressing, until our son, aged nine, read a classified advertisement in the newspaper, rode a bus to town and advised us by telephone that he had invested five dollars, his life's savings, in a dog of uncertain sex and origin. We took it home in the car, and the purchase turned out to be a brown, thickly furred water spaniel bitch with a lady's manners and a grinning, masculine charm.

The owner named her Skipper, and she was always regarded as male. Her—or his—life passed without trouble or a day's illness. Skipper ate no meat, cooked or uncooked, only vegetables, preferably raw cabbages and corn stolen from the garden. They were consumed at leisure on the driveway, while at camp he—or she—enjoyed swimming, sailing and chasing squirrels that were never caught.

After fifteen years, I found Skipper lying peacefully dead under the kitchen table. The noblest of our dogs was buried in the oak grove, and we resolved that there would be no successor to wrench our hearts again.

Like so many others, our resolution failed when my two grandsons arrived on the bus with a living object secreted in the elder boy's coat pocket. They, too, had saved five dollars and bought a shiny black mongrel pup not much larger than a rat but handsomely shaped. As he grew into the dimensions of a miniature Labrador retriever, he was given the name of Nickel to denote his size. But everybody called him Nick. Walking daily with my daughter, he became the friend and familiar of the whole neighbourhood.

After Joan had gone, Nick embraced Gladys Veitch, whose experience with dogs was greater than mine. She treated him and the cat like children, but they no longer belonged to her. By nature's decree she belonged to them.

Nick, investing his life in human, not his own, species, taught me certain verities that he could not suspect. I had come, in my age, to believe that dogs as a rule are more shapely than men or women and more virtuous. Look into the eyes of a good dog and you will glimpse the infinite variety and possibilities of life. You will also be reminded that dog and man travel the same unmarked road to the great unknown, differing only in levels of intelligence by a pretty narrow margin.

At some levels, indeed, the dog is our superior, with senses that we have lost—not just the senses of ear, eye, nose, touch and palate but something far deeper, a method of communication between animal and human minds that physical science cannot fathom. The dog knows the master as well as the master knows the dog.

Look again into the dog's eyes and you will observe their puzzlement, the longing search for reality behind the veil, the insoluble dilemma of all mankind. With his unspoken language,

Nick tells us his pleasures and his doubts. Now he is old, but I hope that his departure may be delayed past mine. For the veterinarian's merciful act of ending a life of pain must bring searing grief to the dog's friends.

Hence its so-called ownership is a grave responsibility when it cannot identify the source of its pain as a baby can, nor choose its owner, nor summon the law's protection against brutal treatment, even torture, in a laboratory. No one except a man or woman reasonably benign—though sinners all—is worthy of a good dog's trust.

Birds, too, were a comfort to us in the dark months. Wild geese, wintering on lakes outside the town, grew restless as daylight increased. They circled overhead as if hesitating to fly north and their guttural croak sounded sweet in nostalgic Canadian ears. Seagulls, riding the wind currents, mewed like kittens. Swarms of hungry birds, including a dozen resident Steller's jays, crowded our feed tables.

One day they were joined by a migrant no larger than a sparrow, with pale blue wings and a robin's breast. Since we had never seen its like, Gladys Veitch phoned the Rare Bird Alert. Its professional ornithologist hurried to our place, focussed his binoculars and made twittering sounds. Nothing happened. The visitor had flown away.

It came back next morning, the ornithologist hurried out again and repeated his twitters, but the quarry had left for good. A coloured picture in our birdbook showed, beyond doubt, that we had entertained a lazuli bunting. The expert said that birds of its kind hardly ever appeared here in winter. Our single contribution to ornithology caused a minor sensation among the town's birdwatchers.

Afterwards, we had to be satisfied with the common run of visitors. Their behaviour reminded us of mankind's habits. Even when we provided more grain than our guests could eat, they fought each other for the surplus supply as nations do. But with birds, a few pecks and flutters are sufficient weapons.

Exciting incidents like the visit of the bunting rarely occurred. For the most part, my habits were tedious. On balance, I judged, old age, though easily achieved if you live long enough, cannot be recommended nor understood by anyone who has not reached it. But, given tolerable health, antiquity bestows blessings as well as horrors.

No longer is it necessary to torment yourself with the unanswerable questions that torment the young, to make judgements on complex public issues when you are ignorant of the facts, to recognize the famous names and scandals of politics and high society headlined on the front pages. But it is necessary, to keep things in proportion, that you remember how world events of one liftime have changed human affairs by a full millennium in history's timetable. And in his own brief experience, a man has passed through many phases drastically changing him, too.

As one who admires Wordsworth, I like to think that, without poetry or intimations of immortality, I have dabbled in his three phases of life—the boy's thoughtless outdoor sport, the young man's passionate, almost carnal, love of nature, and the old man's vision of the dark, inscrutable workmanship, reconciling discordant elements, making them cling together in one society.

If I could not hear Wordsworth's still, sad music, I had witnessed, at least remotely, the discord, the folly and the unspeakable crimes of this enlightened century, and I had come, very late, to understand the wisdom of El Ghazali, the Arabian mystic, who said: "You possess only whatever will not be lost in a shipwreck."

For a little while I possessed, according to man-made law, a tiny fragment of the Canadian earth, and by a law unwritten, the right to observe some of its life forms. Looking out the window today on the field, the valley, the blue hills and, in memory, the cabin and the forest, I regret my own numberless faults but not a life in the country.